RAF LINDIA

Girl in a Glass Box

Published by ill House Publishing – CT.
Cover by Michael Corvin
Photo by Chia Messina – NY

Chapter 1

GROTON, CONNECTICUT
AUGUST 26, 2019

It was eight in the morning when Emily Barton pulled her cream Honda Fit into the parking lot of the Groton Police Station. She turned off the engine and gripped the steering wheel, her gaze fixed on the entrance. Emily took a deep breath and locked eyes with herself for a moment in the rearview mirror; what she saw reflected in her sea-green eyes wasn't quite compassion, but it was close. She freshened up her coral lipstick, and got out of the car. The late-summer day was mild and pleasant.

She stopped at the foot of the few steps leading to the entrance and took another deep breath. Every time she faced that door, she couldn't help but remember the first time she had walked through it, seven years earlier. She shook the disturbing thought from her mind and gazed indifferently at her reflection in the glass door. She smoothed her blond hair, which she wore in a bob, and adjusted her black leather crossbody bag to keep it from snagging the short pink dress she'd chosen for the occasion. She opened the door and entered.

"Emily! What a pleasant surprise!" exclaimed the officer behind the information desk.

The young woman smiled and approached the desk. "Hi, Hank. How are you?"

The man grimaced and patted his rotund belly before responding, "Not great. The wife put me on a strict diet, and she's involving the entire station in this mission of hers to get me to lose thirty pounds. So, now I've got to get my snacks from the vending machine on the downlow."

Emily chuckled. "Well, you're not hiding it very well, Hank. If you don't clean up those crumbs in your beard, you'll be found out very soon."

Looking sheepish, Hank rubbed his hand across his face. "How about now?"

Emily chucked again. "It's perfectly fine, just like before. There weren't any crumbs. I was just joking."

Hank laughed heartily. "You're here to see Peter, I assume," he asked as he picked up the telephone receiver.

"You assume correctly," Emily replied, still smiling.

"I'll call him right away," the officer said, dialing the internal number and smiling up at her. "Peter, there's a lovely young lady here, and she's asking for you. What should I tell her?"

Emily heard faint chatter from the receiver.

"Alright. I'll let her know," Hank concluded, hanging up. "He'll be down in a few minutes. You can sit in the waiting room if you'd like. There's no one here at this hour, and there's also a vending machine if you're interested." Hank winked.

Emily grinned. "Thank you, definitely. Although I suspect all the good snacks might be gone by now." Emily winked back and then headed toward the nearby glass-walled waiting area.

She placed her purse on one of the faux-leather chairs and looked around. One wall bore a panel of missing persons' photos, and Emily approached it, curious to see if there were any new postings. There weren't, but there were still dozens of sheets, immortalizing people of all ages, but mostly women and children. Some were from many years earlier, faded by time. Others were more recent, clearer and in vibrant color. In all of them, people were smiling—a wall of people showing their best smiles. Happy.

Emily simply swept her eyes across the images. She didn't examine them too closely; it would be too painful to put names to the faces. She couldn't help but think that that wall of smiles was a grim contradiction, considering the reasons for which these photos were displayed. These people may have been killed, perhaps sexually abused or tortured, or had escaped from unsafe family situations. Some had gone missing ten years earlier, some even twenty. Emily's eyes unwittingly rested on the photo of a little brown-haired boy who had disappeared in 1986 at age five.

Thirty-three years of searching, without any answers, she thought, as a shiver ran down her spine. She felt sorry for the boy's family, for all the families between the lines of these missing persons posters.

"Sad, isn't it?" came Peter's voice from behind, startling her.

She turned and embraced him before returning her gaze to the wall. "Yes, very sad," she whispered. "So many children, young girls, and teenagers."

"And these are just the missing persons in Groton and Mystic," Peter replied soberly. "If I were to show you the dossier of those from the entire state, you'd be horrified."

"Some are found, yes?" Emily asked. "I mean, do you manage to locate *any* of them?"

Peter lowered his gaze and put his hands in his pants pockets. "We find some of them. One percent. But, in most cases, we find them dead. Sometimes, by chance, while walking in the woods, someone reports seeing a pile of bones in the bushes. Other times, an anonymous tip directs us to where they were killed and buried. To be honest, in my career, however short it may be, we've never brought anyone back alive. Once they go missing, unless it's a voluntary escape, there isn't much hope of finding them alive."

Peter Avellino was twenty-seven years old and had recently joined the police force, following in the footsteps of his dad, a detective. Tall, slim, with curly black hair, Peter had grown up in the nearby town of Madison with his adoptive Italian-American parents. He and Emily had met during a trying time in the young woman's life and had fallen in love at some point within their seven years of friendship. And that past June, following Emily's graduation with a PharmD degree, to her delight, Peter had proposed to her at her small graduation party. He'd knelt down and presented her with a small, square-cut diamond ring. With happy tears in her eyes, Emily had readily accepted.

The couple had planned a brief engagement, but two weeks later, Emily had received a job offer at Pfizer on the condition she move to their office in Kalamazoo, Michigan—an amazing opportunity for the career-minded girl, fresh out of college, who had always dreamed of being a pharmaceutical researcher. So the couple decided to postpone setting a wedding date, with the hope that, within a few years, Emily could transfer to Pfizer's New York headquarters, which was only two hours from Groton, Connecticut, and Peter's job. In the meantime, they agreed to a long-distance engagement with visits as frequent as their schedules would allow.

"Let's talk about something else, my love," Peter suggested, putting his arm around her shoulders. "Are you ready?"

"Let's say yes," she replied.

Peter turned to meet her eye. “Are you sure you don’t want me to come inside with you?” he asked. “If you’d rather do it on your own, I totally respect that, but I—”

“I’m sure,” she cut him off. “Just knowing you’re nearby will give me strength. But first, I’d like to stop by the cemetery, if you’re okay with that. This will be my last opportunity for a while.”

“Of course, my love. In Mystic?”

“Yes, the Elm Grove Cemetery.”

Peter and Emily headed toward the exit, hand in hand.

“Treat that gem well, Avellino!” Hank shouted from behind his desk.

Without turning around, Peter raised his thumb to the sky. Emily smiled and gripped Peter’s other hand tightly as they passed through the glass door.

* * *

Emily rode in the passenger seat as Peter steered her car along the tree-lined dirt road that ran through the Elm Grove Cemetery.

After about fifty feet of driving at a snail’s pace, Emily whispered, “Here. Stop here.”

Peter hit the brake and looked around. The small cemetery was situated on the bank of the Mystic River, and although it was usually quite busy on Sundays, at that early hour, there were only a few people walking among the various gravestones to visit their departed loved ones.

Emily got out of the car and removed her shoes to avoid sinking their sharp heels into the dew-dampened ground. She took a few steps and stopped in front of a dark granite headstone.

Her bare feet sank into the grass as she gazed at the grave, barely perceiving the warmth of Peter's presence a few steps behind her.

The stone bore the inscription ROBERT SMITH, OCTOBER 28, 1996 TO MAY 26, 2012.

Emily gently placed a hand on the cold granite and bowed her head. After a moment, she crouched to brush away a clump of dry weeds at the base of the stone and rearranged the still-fresh flowers someone must have placed there not long ago.

"Did you love him?" Peter asked, still standing.

Emily smiled without turning around. Her voice barely rose above a whisper, and she never took her eyes off the framed photo of the young man on the headstone. "Well, he was my first crush. I was sure what I felt was love, but Robert and I were so young. We met on the first day of school in our senior year. He'd just moved to Mystic from somewhere in England. I didn't know he was interested in me, but then, as I've told you, one day, he gave me that gift." She felt her face flush in remembrance. "That's how it all started. Then, two weeks before the prom, he asked me to go with him. Well, you know all this . . . and how he turned up here."

Peter approached and placed a hand on her shoulder. "You don't have to feel responsible for what happened."

The young woman offered the still air another faint smile. "I know . . . I'm not," she replied, caressing the stone and running her fingers over the engraved letters of the young man's name. "But I struggle not to. He'd still be alive if I'd turned down that invitation and we hadn't gone to the prom together. He would have graduated and most likely become a successful pharmaceutical researcher in California, as he had planned. He would have been happy. Instead, he's here."

Peter gently squeezed her shoulder.

Emily stood up without taking her eyes off the grim reminder and took a deep breath. “It’s time to go,” she said, taking her fiancé’s hand. “I don’t want to be late.”

Peter gave her hand a tight squeeze as a long shadow fell over them and a shrill voice demanded from behind, “What are *you* doing here?”

Peter turned with a startle toward the voice, but Emily remained impassive, her head down.

“I told you never to come here again!” the woman added irately.

Emily turned slowly, and, without making eye contact with the raging, middle-aged woman, she walked toward the car, pulling Peter along.

From her periphery, Emily could see the woman shaking the bunch of flowers in her hand toward her as if they were a weapon.

“Aren’t you ashamed at all?” the woman continued, her English accent becoming more pronounced. “After what you did? Go back where you came from and never dare to set foot here again! You even profited from my son’s death. I’ll tell you again . . . don’t ever come see Robert again, never! And, you, young man! If you value your life, stay away from that girl!”

Emily didn’t look at her, didn’t respond, and briskly walked to the car’s passenger door. She opened it and climbed into the seat, head bowed, as Peter got into the driver’s seat.

Peter started the car and sped off after a quick look in the rearview mirror. He let out the breath he was holding. “That was_”

“Please, Peter,” Emily begged without raising her head. “Don’t speak.”

Peter obeyed and drove the car out of the cemetery, then turned onto the interstate leading to I-95 and headed south. Emily did not utter a word for the thirty-minute drive to Niantic. Hurt beyond words by the woman's never-ending animosity toward her, she let a single tear roll down her face.

* * *

It was exactly ten o'clock when Emily and Peter parked in the visitor's area of the York Women's Prison. The compound consisted of a series of single-story, slope-roofed concrete structures overlooking the water of Bride Lake, a natural lake just under a thousand square feet in size. There were no trees around the facility, and the existing greenery was poorly maintained and parched by the summer heat.

It was only when they arrived that Emily raised her gaze and stared at the entrance through the windshield. "I'm sorry, Peter," she murmured. "I didn't mean to be rude. I never imagined she'd be at the cemetery at the precise time I was visiting. I mean, what are the chances? Anyway, if I had suspected, I wouldn't have gone, and I would have spared you the embarrassment."

Peter took Emily's hand and looked at her. "Oh, Emily, you're not responsible for what happened. She's clearly still grieving the loss of her son, and she doesn't know how to be anything but angry at you. It isn't fair of her."

Emily didn't respond, instead she asked, "Why are you with me? My life is a constant disaster. It's cursed. Anyone who has gotten close to me has suffered. Maybe Robert's mother is right. If you value your life, it would be better for you to stay away from me."

Peter squeezed her hand tightly, his expression turning serious. "Don't even joke about that, Emily. None of your misfortune has been your fault. Anyway, you've done great things with your life, and you know what else? Your life as *Mrs.* Avellino will be happy and fulfilling. I promise."

Emily met his reassuring smile, returned it, and clasped his hand with both of hers. "Thank you, Peter. I do love you so much." She kissed him on the lips, lingering for just a moment to appreciate his closeness. Then, reluctantly but resolutely, she turned her gaze back to the entrance of the penitentiary and took a deep breath. *Okay. Let's do this.* She opened the car door.

"I'll be here waiting for you, my love," Peter said from the driver's seat.

Emily smiled at him without responding and headed inside. At the door, a dark-skinned female security officer directed Emily to the visitor check-in booth.

"Prisoner to visit?" the officer asked, and her gaze fixed on the logbook she had on the counter.

"Valerie Davidson Barton," Emily replied.

"And you are?" the officer asked.

"Emily Barton," the young woman answered, showing her driver's license to the officer.

"Relationship to the inmate?"

"I'm her daughter," Emily said, her voice cracking.

The policewoman raised her eyes and stared at Emily. She handed Emily a visitor's sticker and had her sign the logbook. "Please wait in the waiting room to the right." She indicated a wooden door on the side of the check-in area. "We'll call you when the inmate is ready."

Emily looked for an available chair in the waiting room. There were about twenty people waiting to visit someone. She took a seat on an uncomfortable gray plastic chair in the corner opposite the door. On the left, behind a protective glass, another female officer, this one with curly blond hair and age-revealing gray roots and weathered skin, was calling out the names of people permitted into the visiting area. Next to her was a barred door with an electronic lock.

"Stevenson!" the officer shouted.

A bald man, who had been engrossed in reading a gardening magazine, stood up abruptly and winced. Rubbing his lower back, he approached the glass. The man showed his ID to the officer, who unlocked the door next to the check-in booth.

"Empty your pockets in one of the available lockers," the officer instructed him, pointing out what to do, "and pass under the metal detector. A colleague will escort you to the visiting area."

Emily remained seated, observing the scene. She'd experienced the exchange dozens of times over the years. Her mother, Valerie, had been incarcerated in that prison for nearly seven years, and since then, Emily had dutifully visited her twice a month. However, today's visit was different from the others. Emily had come to inform her mother about the exciting progress she'd made with regard to her dream career, and, knowing her mother, Valerie wouldn't take the news well.

Lost in these thoughts and searching for the right words, Emily sat with her hands on her knees, waiting to be called. Her right leg bounced nervously. She clenched it tightly to stop it but with no success. So, she took a deep breath and held it four a count of four to regain her calm. Staring at the scuffed floor, her eyes settling on a chipped, scratched white tile nearby. Without taking her eyes off it, she began to count slowly, and quietly. "One, two, three, four, five, six, seven, eight, nine, ten . . ." Emily whispered, then started again, interspersing the series with three deep breaths. "One, two, three . . ." She had counted almost six series when she heard the female officer shouting her name. "Barton!"

Emily stood up and approached the glass counter. "I'm Emily Barton," she said to the officer, who then opened the barred door by pressing a button.

"Empty your pockets in one of the available lockers. You should also leave your purse. After passing through the metal detector, an officer will escort you to the visiting area."

"Thank you," Emily replied, crossing the metal threshold.

Once inside the inspection room, she placed her purse into a blue locker with a combination lock; the pink dress had no pockets to empty. She always used the same sequence of numbers to secure the lock—0910, her date of birth, September 10.

She could feel the officer in the room closely watching her every move. When Emily had closed and secured the locker, the guard signaled for her to proceed under the metal detector.

Emily slowly stepped through the electronic frame, which lit up green as she passed through it. The officer nodded in approval to her colleague behind the second barred door, who immediately opened the door and pulled it toward herself, allowing Emily to pass.

Beyond, Emily found herself in a too-familiar room with dozens of wooden tables, each with two chairs facing each other. Almost all were occupied by a visitor facing a woman dressed in a brick-red T-shirt, the color of the uniforms for inmates at York Women's Prison.

Valerie Barton was waiting at one of the tables. She was a near-perfect copy of Emily, only much older and marked by life.

Valerie had unkempt blond hair, full lips, and sea-green eyes. She also wore the red uniform T-shirt. Upon seeing her, her mother stood up, her face lighting up with a smile that revealed teeth yellowed by too many cigarettes.

Emily gave a small smile as she approached. Valerie sat back down and gestured toward the chair in front, inviting her daughter to sit. Physical contact was not allowed, and the table was over four feet wide to keep the inmate and visitor as far apart as possible. Even though the temptation to hold hands was strong during these visits, whenever such a thing happened, one of the guards stationed in the four corners of the room would immediately shout the inmate's name to reprimand them.

Emily took her seat in front of her mother and suppressed a sigh.

"My little flower, how are you?" Valerie asked.

"I'm fine, Mom," Emily replied. "How about you?"

Valerie leaned back in her chair and spread her arms. "How can I be? In this hell? Surrounded by thieves and blasphemers? I'm surviving, but I can't wait for the day of my appeal hearing."

Emily bowed her head over the table, grimacing at the thought that the verdict from seven years earlier could be reconsidered, as unlikely as that would be. "Mom, I've come to talk to you about something very important," Emily said, staring at a scratch in the corner of the table.

Valerie froze and leaned on the table, staring at her daughter. "Is something wrong, honey? I can see you're troubled."

Emily paused. She knew her mother's personality well. Valerie wouldn't respond calmly to the news she had to deliver. Emily was practically terrified to give it to her. "Mom, I have some good news. It's about my career," she said almost in one breath.

Valerie smiled a smile that Emily knew well. False. Stiff. Concerned. The woman's lips had immediately thinned as she tried to show positivity. But her nervousness showed in that small tremor at the corner of her mouth. Emily knew her mother was not a woman who liked changes and that what was good news for Emily could be bad news for her.

"Tell me, Emily! What is it?" Valerie asked, smiling with feigned sweetness. "Don't tell me you've already found a job you like?"

"Yes, Mom," Emily replied, trying to conceal her nervousness. "Not only a job that I really like, but it's with one of the biggest pharmaceutical companies in the world. An amazing opportunity for me."

Valerie's smile tightened and her eyes went wide, as if she were surprised and impressed by the news. "And *where* is this job?"

The question Emily dreaded the most had finally been asked. She lowered her head again, glanced at another point on the table, and steeled herself. "In Michigan," she replied almost in a whisper. "At Pfizer's laboratory."

At first, Valerie stared at her daughter without any reaction. After a few seconds, her gaze locked with Emily's. Through that gaze, Emily could practically hear her mother's thoughts: *Moving to Michigan meant no more bimonthly visits. It meant Emily would be going far away. It meant Emily would be independent.*

"How far is Michigan?" Valerie asked with false calmness.

"About a two-hour flight from New York," Emily whispered.

Valerie clenched her hands together on the tabletop and lowered her gaze to stare at them as if she were crushing something between her palms. "Two hours by flight. And then the drive from New York to here? Another two and a half hours or so. Do you know what that means, Emily?" she asked without looking up. "It means that after *everything* I've done for you, you're leaving me to rot in this hellhole, alone."

"Mom," Emily tried to intervene.

"Mom, nothing. You *can't* leave me here. You *can't* possibly be *that* selfish," Valerie nearly yelled.

"This is an opportunity of a lifetime," Emily protested. "I couldn't have dreamed of a better start to my career."

"Dreams?" Valerie asked, staring at her daughter as red patches of anger bloomed on her face. "What do you think of *my* dreams—the ones that were shattered to raise you, take care of you, protect you? What about those? All broken and gone, only to end up in this place."

Emily lowered her gaze. She understood what was happening here, and she knew she had to respond. She wouldn't let this guilt trip keep her from embracing her opportunity at Pfizer. "It's not my fault you're here," she replied calmly.

"It's for you that I'm here," Valerie retorted. "To protect you. To cover up your problems. To spare you other people's harsh judgment. To spare you from suffering—and you know it!"

Emily clenched her teeth, trying to gather her strength. She had come here to tell her mother about her decision, to share with her what should have been considered good news. She had done it knowing and expecting this reaction. And she had prepared herself for it.

"Mom," Emily said firmly, "nothing will change my mind. I've made up my mind. I've accepted the job, and in a few days, I'm leaving for Michigan. And I would like, for once, for you to be happy for me."

Valerie leapt to her feet. "You're not going anywhere!" she shouted, attracting the attention of one of the guards.

"Volume!" one of the women in uniform shouted.

"You promised!" Valerie raged, staring down at Emily's bowed head. "You promised you would stand by me. That you would stay with me until I could get out of this place! You have no gratitude, young lady. You have no shame, and, most importantly, you have no guilt!"

Hearing those words, Emily raised her head and stared gravely up at her mother. "You can't say this to me."

"Silence! I don't want to hear another word! I want you to leave and think better about what you're planning to do. You know you're doing something wrong. You know I would die in here knowing you're far away and not even having that little bit you give me with these visits twice a month. If you decide to go away, you'll kill me!" Valerie concluded before gesturing to the guard to indicate that the visit was over.

Emily remained seated, silently watching her mother disappear through the door leading to the cells, walking tall and without looking back.

Several seconds passed before another guard gestured to Emily that it was time to leave the visiting room.

Emily stood, troubled by her mother's words, by those accusations that, over the years, had sometimes been disguised as tender words and at other times had been pronounced directly. She had spent her years in college shuttling between the campus, the prison, and her therapist's office. She had always been there for her Mother these past seven years, despite it all. But now it was time to take control of her own life. It was time to think about her future—to leave behind the wounded past for what life had in store for her future.

Emily walked toward the exit, weighed down by the realization that this visit would be the last of her bimonthly visits.

As she crossed the parking lot, Peter exited the car and hurried over to her.

She let him hug her and let herself cry in her fiancé's arms. They stood wrapped in each other's arms in a silence broken only by Emily's sobs.

When her sobs were spent, the couple got back in the car. Emily kept quiet as Peter started the engine and set off again toward the highway, heading north once more, toward Mystic.

"Do you want to talk about it?" Peter asked, breaking the silence.

Emily lowered her gaze. "I guess. There's not a lot to say. I told her that I'm leaving, and she took it like she takes everything badly," Emily replied, turning her eyes back to the road ahead.

Peter nodded in understanding. "Are you sure you want to go to your old house today? Haven't you had enough of the past for one day? You can take a break if you want."

"No," she replied. "We need to close this chapter before I can take my next step toward the future. Take me to Mystic. Please."

They fell silent.

Emily lost herself in her thoughts, reflecting on her mother's words, on the guilt that Valerie was so adept at making her feel ever since she was a little girl. Emily knew this sense of guilt shouldn't have been hers to carry, but she couldn't shake it from her being. It had seeped into her, becoming part of her very identity. Emily had grown up with that feeling, and since that cursed day seven years earlier, she had felt imprisoned, too guilty, in an invisible prison haunted by ghosts. And she felt that the time had come to finally free herself, to try to rid herself of all the pain and confusion and leave those ghouls behind.

She looked over at Peter, her handsome, loving fiancée. He knew her backstory, the suffering she had endured, and what she was experiencing now. She had no doubt that he loved her. They had met when she was vulnerable and wounded, and he had stood by her through her fight to normalcy. Piece by piece, she had rebuilt her life. A new life. A life free of the victimhood that had colored her past. Peter often reminded Emily that she was strong and that he loved her for that, too. He must have felt her looking at him because he reached out and placed his hand on her leg.

Emily took his hand in hers and smiled. "Thank you," she whispered. "I couldn't have made such progress without your support. I love you, Peter Avellino."

"I love you too, Emily," the young man replied. "I'm here if you want to talk." When a few minutes passed without another word from Emily, Peter turned on the radio to fill the silence, and Emily lost herself in the music.

Within the hour, they arrived at the vacant house where Emily had grown up. The small property, which was still owned by her mother even though taxes were somewhat in arrears, was located on Morgan Street in the west part of town. It was a small, white house with a red-tiled roof and stood nestled in a quarter acre of land now overtaken by scrub and brambles.

As Peter turned off the engine, Emily turned her gaze toward the house, examining it as if it were the first time she had seen it. It had been seven years since she had last closed that white aluminum door behind her, but Emily remembered it well. Despite the overgrowth, the erosion of the bricks of the two entrance steps, and the shattered state of the white picket fence, every corner of that structure and its history were etched clearly in the young woman's memory.

The garage was closed, and on the door frame, a small piece of frayed yellow police tape fluttered in the breeze, as if to remind anyone passing by of the dramatic events that had unfolded on the property. She remembered her father's blue pickup truck parked inside. She recalled the acrid smell of ammonia and gasoline, the green plastic tarp in the truck bed, with mud on the wheels and sides.

"It looks like a haunted house," she whispered without taking her eyes off her former home.

"In a way, it is," Peter replied softly. "And I still think you should leave the ghosts in there to rot."

"I know, my love. I just need to spend a few minutes, and then we'll leave," she said as she grabbed the door handle.

Emily and Peter walked through the small gate and approached the house slowly. Peter looked around curiously; Emily kept her head down.

Reaching the door, Emily dug the key out of her purse and inserted it into the rusted lock. She had trouble opening it, so Peter gave the door a shove as she turned the key. The door swung open noisily, shifting the stagnant air inside and sending a cloud of dust into the air. Peter gestured for Emily to lead the way inside. She crossed the threshold, trying to contain her agitation.

It took a few moments to adjust to the darkness. The front door of the house opened into the living room. Peter attempted to turn on the light with no success; there was no electricity, so the young man opened the curtains of the window facing the street.

Emily stood still in the center of the room, looking around. It was as if time had stood still. Everything was still in its place–the sofa, the reclining armchair where her father used to sit and watch TV, the coffee table in the middle with a glass vase containing what remained of a bouquet of flowers, whose dried and yellowed leaves lay scattered on the table, while the petrified stems were still upright, missing their now-incinerated bulbs.

Peter placed a hand on her shoulder. "Shall we continue?" he whispered.

Emily nodded, and she headed toward the kitchen, with Peter following closely behind.

"I don't quite remember where my mother kept my documents," the young woman said as she began to open the drawers of a small, glass cabinet.

Peter continued to look around, palpably intrigued. He moved slowly, examining everything closely. Emily glanced up to see him studying the wall behind the dining table, on which still hung some photos hanging depicting Emily as a child, accompanied by her mother. She was smiling in those pictures. In one, she sat at the edge of a swimming pool. Another showed the two of them side by side as Emily blew out a "number 9" candle on a chocolate cake. Another photo showed Emily dressed in her school uniform, gap-toothed and smiling.

"You were a beautiful child," Peter said staring at the photos.

"Thank you," Emily replied without pausing her rummaging.

The Pfizer hiring office had requested the original copy of her Social Security card, and Emily hadn't seen it since her school days. She hadn't needed it in intervening years, but she knew the card must still be in that house. Yes, it would have been easier for her to go to the Social Security office to request a replacement card, but something kept her from taking the easy way out. Deep down, she wanted to put her memories of this place to rest before she moved to Michigan.

Having had no luck in the kitchen drawers, Emily headed toward the stairs leading to the upper floor. Peter followed her.

The upper floor consisted of a small bedroom, a bathroom, and a spacious storage room. Emily's parents' bedroom was on the lower floor. They entered Emily's childhood bedroom. Peter gazed around as if he were in a museum, but Emily immediately began to rifle through the dresser drawers and those of the nightstand next to the bed. Nothing there had any sentimental value to her.

On the wall in front of the bed hung a poster depicting the periodic table. The wall next to it bore only a photo of Emily and her mother in front of a church.

There were no old dolls or anything else. Just a few schoolbooks and a bulky laptop on a small desk. It didn't seem like the room where a young girl had grown up. It was as if it had no personality at all.

Sad, Emily thought distantly. *Only that periodic table.* Her destiny had been imprinted on that wall for years. One destiny. One goal. No other distractions or interests.

She could sense Peter's unease and was sure she knew what he was thinking. Emily had never had a childhood—not the childhood of a normal girl with her things. There were no posters of her idol on the wall, no Polaroids or photobooth strips of her with her best friend. No postcard from a city she might have visited on a school trip. None of that. This room further clarified what she had already told him about her life. About her loneliness. About her being different and isolated.

Emily let out an impatient huff. "I can't find it!" she exclaimed as she emptied the small drawers onto the bed.

"Maybe it's in the master bedroom," Peter suggested.

"Yeah, maybe," she replied impatiently and headed back downstairs with Peter on her heels.

Valerie's bedroom was small, populated by a double bed, a classic-style dresser with a mirror above it, two nightstands, and a small closet.

The bed was messy, and some drawers were fully open or poorly closed. The room clearly showed signs of a police search. By the grim look on Peter's face, Emily knew he had seen such a scene many times while working alongside police investigators.

Emily looked around without touching anything, staring at the dresser as if hypnotized. Her mind drifted back to the last time she had opened the drawers of that piece of furniture. She could feel Peter staring at her. She had told him the whole story, and now that they were within these walls, he must have understood even better what had happened. The nuances of that story that not even Emily could fully detail lay in the scattered details in these rooms.

Emily rummaged through her mother's drawers as best as she could but found no trace of the sought-after document. So, she stopped and looked around, lost in thought. "There's one more place it could be," she said, leaving the room without looking at Peter. She heard his footsteps following as she headed toward the basement door.

The basement was dim, lit only by two small windows that, due to the overgrown grass outside, barely illuminated the room. On one wall, a metal shelving unit held sealed cardboard boxes. Emily took down one with her name written on it. She placed it on the ground, knelt down, and opened it.

As she poked through the box, she glanced up occasionally at Peter, who peered around at the boxes and various items littering the space. There was an old sewing machine, a wooden radio from the 1950s, and an old cathode-ray tube television. In one corner stood a metal desk with three drawers. Each drawer had a yellowed paper label; one said "projects," the second "contracts," and the third "taxes." This was the desk where Emily's father had kept his work documents.

In the corner of the room, in an area dimly lit by the outside light, was a wooden door, held shut by a safety clasp and secured by a broken padlock. Peter now stared at the door. Emily had told him where it led, and he seemed to recall it then; he visibly shuddered. Emily turned her eyes back to the box, heart pounding, and–

"Found it!" she shouted, springing to her feet.

Peter jumped, then turned and hugged her. "Great. I'm glad."

"Okay, love," Emily said, kissing Peter on the lips. "Now we can leave this creepy place. What do you say?"

Peter glanced at the wooden door with the padlock. "Is that the room?" he asked, visibly embarrassed.

Emily turned to face the door. "Yes. That's it."

A few seconds of silence passed as both stared at the entrance.

"Can I see it?" Peter asked.

Emily took a moment to reflect. She wasn't thrilled about the idea of revisiting what was behind that door. The truth of her life. Everything she had experienced in those years was explained by what was in that room, a realization that had haunted her ever since she had entered it for the first and only time seven years earlier. Now, Peter was asking her to relive that experience. But Emily was no longer afraid. She had decided that the ghosts and the memory of those tragic events could no longer harm her.

"If you insist, okay," she replied, determined.

Peter approached slowly and removed the broken padlock. He pushed the small door inward, and it creaked eerily as it swung open.

The young man took a step forward and crossed the threshold, while Emily remained outside the room, watching him. She knew what she had told him didn't do justice to the image before him, to the sadness she felt rippling off him as he gazed around.

"Oh my God!" Peter exclaimed.

Chapter 2

MYSTIC, CONNECTICUT
AUGUST 11, 2001

The sound of the front door slamming startled Emily from her sleep.

The little girl opened her eyes and checked the small alarm clock on her nightstand. It was half past six in the morning. Emily frowned and turned over in bed, intending to go back to sleep. But only a few minutes passed before the sound of someone sobbing penetrated her doze.

Emily opened her eyes again and looked around. She got out of bed, put on her fuzzy slippers, and went into the hallway. She listened for a moment and realized that the crying was coming from downstairs.

She descended the stairs, trying not to make any noise. When she reached the last step, Emily stumbled over a pair of muddy garden boots. The child froze, hoping no one had heard. But the crying didn't stop, and Emily realized it was coming from the kitchen. So she continued down the hallway until she stood in the kitchen doorway.

Her mother, Valerie, sat slumped at the dining table, tears streaming down her face, holding papers in one hand and a burning cigarette in the other.

"Mom?" Emily whispered.

Valerie turned, crushed out her cigarette in the overflowing ashtray, and folded the papers. She wiped her red-rimmed eyes with the back of her hand. "What are you doing up at this hour?" she asked, opening her arms to beckon Emily closer.

The little girl approached and let herself be embraced. Valerie hugged her tightly.

"Mom, you're squeezing me too hard!" Emily complained.

Her mother released her. "I'm sorry, honey. It's just that I'm so happy to see you," she said, pulling another Marlboro from the box on the table.

"Why are you crying?"

Valerie lowered her gaze and lit her cigarette. She took a deep inhale. The smoke blew from her mouth as she spoke, "There's something important you need to know, honey. But first, I want you to know that I love you more than my own life."

"Something important?" Emily intoned.

Valerie remained silent for a few moments. "Sit here," she said at last, tapping the chair beside her.

Emily obeyed, sat down, and stared at her mother.

"Your father has decided to leave us," Valerie whispered.

Emily frowned, confused. "Leave us? Where is he going?"

Valerie smiled gently. "I don't know where. But he's left us."

Emily tried to process those words. Her father had gone? Forever? "When did he leave?" she asked as tears welled up in her eyes.

Valerie caressed the child's face and sighed. "This morning. Very early. And he won't be coming back. He says he doesn't want to be with us anymore."

Emily looked at her mother, baffled, and then looked at the folded papers on the table. Though Emily wasn't even six years old yet, she was very perceptive. Her mind went back to the night before, to her father's cuddles before bedtime, to the words he had spoken to her as he tucked her in. "You're my precious pearl," he had told her before arranging her blankets and kissing her on the forehead.

Now he was gone. Without saying goodbye. *Was that meant to be his farewell?* she wondered. "What are those papers? A letter?" she asked, still looking at the table.

Valerie's gaze followed her daughter's. She seemed to contemplate for a moment before answering. "Yes, honey," she responded at last. "Your father left us a letter before he left."

"Can you read it to me?" Emily begged, her vision swimming in tears. "Does it say why he left? Was it because you always fought?"

Valerie left her cigarette burning in the ashtray to grab the papers; she held them tightly to her chest. "It will hurt too much for you to read it. Yes, we fought a lot. But I can tell you that your father loves you. He had his reasons for leaving, and you need to stay calm. *I,* on the other hand, will *never* leave you, and no one will ever take you away from me. I'll take care of you. I'll be both your mom and dad from now on."

Valerie hugged her child tightly, but Emily remained limp, feeling as if she had lost all strength.

Several moments passed before Valerie released her grip and stood up. "Today, you deserve a real princess breakfast," she said, tying a stained kitchen apron around her waist. "Go get dressed while I whip something up!"

Emily slowly made her way out of the room, stopping at the edge of the kitchen, and looked back. Her mother had already left the room through the opposite doorway and had taken that letter with her. Through the open door of Valerie's bedroom, Emily heard the sound of a drawer opening, a shuffling and rustling of papers, and the drawer slamming shut. A moment later, Valerie reentered the kitchen with a startled look. "Emily, I told you to go get yourself ready."

With that, Emily dragged herself upstairs to get dressed.

Emily put on her pink dress, her father's favorite, as if that gesture could magically bring him home. But her mother's words echoed in her head: "Your father has left us forever . . . forever . . . forever."

The girl couldn't believe it. She had often heard her parents fight, but she had never imagined her father, Albert, would leave them forever without saying goodbye, without telling her where he was going and if he would ever come back to see her. Emily felt scared, confused, and lost.

Once dressed, she went downstairs and headed to the door leading to the garage. Her father's blue pickup truck was still there, parked. It was a positive sign, the child reasoned. He couldn't have gone far without his truck.

Emily rushed into the kitchen. "Mom, Mom! Dad's truck is still in the garage!" she exclaimed hopefully. "Maybe he didn't leave forever. Maybe he'll come back! Maybe he was just angry!"

Valerie smiled sadly at her daughter and then caressed her cheek. "Maybe you're right. Maybe he'll come back. But for now, sit down and eat. After breakfast, we'll go for a walk."

Emily devoured the syrupy silver-dollar pancakes made with colorful "princess" sprinkles while gazing at Charlie, her new baby doll, which was sitting on a small chair in the corner of the kitchen. Just a few days earlier, her father had surprised her by coming home with that doll, and since then, she had played with it every day.

Emily's mother sat down beside her daughter, stroked her hair, and smiled at her. "I know you're confused, and I know how much you are hurting. But don't you worry. I will *always* protect you. I will *never* leave you. I will *always* be here for you."

Emily lifted her head and gave a small smile in response.

* * *

The next morning, as soon as Emily woke up, she ran down the stairs to check if her father's truck was still parked in its spot. She knew how much he loved that truck. She remembered the day he had bought it, just eleven months earlier. He had been so proud and excited, behaving like a child. He had let Emily sit on his lap and steer the truck down the road in front of their house. For Emily, that truck represented a flicker of hope for her father's return. She checked for it every day, and soon seven days had passed since her father had gone missing. It was Saturday again, and the car was still there, parked in the same spot. And her father still had not returned.

The hopeful child moved into the kitchen, where she found her mother busy preparing breakfast. Like every Saturday, there were pancakes and maple syrup waiting for her. These pancakes did not have sprinkles.

Emily sat at the table and pushed the ashtray away from her place setting. She was used to the smell, but preferred not to smell it so close while she ate. She turned toward the small chair where she kept Charlie when she wasn't playing with him. But that morning, the doll wasn't in its usual place. "Mom, have you seen Charlie?" the girl asked.

"No, honey," her mother replied without turning away from the stove.

"But I left him there," Emily said, pointing to the empty chair. "On his chair. Where could he have gone?"

Valerie turned and approached her daughter. "I'm sure you left him in your room," she said, with a gentle hand on her shoulder. "We'll go upstairs and look for Charlie together. But first, you must promise me that you'll smile and eat your pancakes."

Emily nodded in agreement. She rushed through breakfast, then scrambled out of her chair and headed upstairs, followed by her mother.

They searched everywhere, starting with Emily's room. Emily called out to her doll as if it could answer her. "Charlie? Charlie, where are you?"

Valerie got down on all fours to check under the bed and beneath the dresser, then stood up and placed her hands on her hips. "Well, maybe you left Charlie somewhere else. Perhaps outside in the garden or in the living room?"

Emily continued searching, inspecting the drawers and the built-in wardrobe. "Charlie and I only play in the kitchen and here in my room," Emily replied, frustrated. "I never take him outside so he won't get dirty."

Valerie spread her arms. "I don't know what to tell you, honey. But don't worry," she said with an uncertain smile. "We'll find him. When you least expect it, Charlie will appear somewhere, and the mystery will be solved."

Emily's head drooped in dismay. She had become attached to that little doll. Charlie was her favorite toy and the last gift she had received from her father.

Mother and daughter descended to the ground floor and sat at the kitchen table, facing each other. Valerie chain-smoked and watched Emily eat in silence.

Emily couldn't stop wondering what had happened to her beloved doll. Suddenly a hopeful thought struck her. "Maybe Charlie is in the basement," she said half-heartedly.

Her mother grinned. "Maybe . . . let's go check."

They descended into the basement and searched in every corner, from the shelves filled with boxes to the space housing the boiler and heating system of the house. Nothing.

"Mom, there's a locked door here!" exclaimed the little girl, pointing at a small wooden door. "Maybe he's in there."

"No, honey," Valerie replied gently. "That room has been locked since before your father left. And I believe he took with him the only key that can open it."

Emily's heart filled with despair, and she resigned herself to the fact that Charlie was gone, just like her father.

* * *

Later that afternoon, Valerie took Emily for a walk in the center of the small town. That August Saturday, Mystic was bustling with tourists from all over the state. The main street, the drawbridge, and the marina were favorite destinations for visitors. Outside the famous Mystic Pizza, a location made famous by the Julia Roberts's film of the same name, a line of people stretched along the entire perimeter of the establishment every weekend.

Mother and daughter walked hand in hand down Library Street to West Main Street. Emily loved that walk to the town center, captivated by the elegant colonial-style houses lining both sides of the street. Emily gazed at them with curiosity and dreamed that, one day, she and her family would live in one of those houses. Her father would return rich from a famous expedition and take them away from their small house on Morgan Street. She would have a room with an old oak tree outside the window, into which she could climb to lie on one of its thick branches to read a book, just like in the movies she watched with her mother after dinner.

However, Valerie was a seamstress, while Emily's father was a plumber. Thanks to her father's income, the family had managed to save some money in anticipation of buying a new house. But now, if her father didn't return, Emily knew Valerie would have to support them with only the meager earnings she made as a seamstress. At least, that's what Emily had overheard her saying on the phone the night before to her aunt Anna.

They arrived on West Main Street and headed for the historic Mystic Drawbridge Ice Cream parlor. Emily loved to eat ice cream while sitting on a bench, waiting to see the spectacular lifting of the bridge as sailboats passed through.

Valerie led Emily inside the ice cream parlor. While Valerie paid for the two ice creams, Emily stared at an almond-studded chocolate bar on display near the cash register.

Valerie glanced down and smiled, then added the chocolate bar to the bill. "But I'll hold on to it for now," Valerie said. "When we get home and after helping me with some chores, you can have it."

Emily smiled enthusiastically. "Thanks, Mom!" she exclaimed as she trotted toward the shop's exit.

Mother and daughter sat in front of the drawbridge, eating their ice creams and watching the passersby, and less than ten minutes passed when the alarm bell signaled the beginning of the lifting procedure. The sun was so hot that Emily's vanilla ice cream melted faster than she could lick it, causing it to drip between her fingers and onto her hand. Emily turned to her mother with excitement, and they shared a smile before they returned their gaze to the simple yet fascinating spectacle of exceptional engineering.

"Mom, do you think Dad will come back to us?" Emily asked after a while. "That he's just angry with you but will come back?"

Valerie's somber eyes remained fixed on the fully raised bridge. "Honey, I know you miss your father. But you shouldn't dwell on it too much. I don't think he'll come back, given the note he left, but if he does, that's good. Otherwise, you and I will be just fine." She hinted at a smile, raising her ice cream as if in a toast.

Emily smiled and did the same.

* * *

Once they returned home, Emily helped her mother fold the fabrics Valerie had purchased that day for some commissioned work. Once they finished, Valerie opened her purse in search of the chocolate bar she had promised to give her daughter. Her expression grew puzzled. "Emily! Did you take the chocolate bar from my purse?"

Wide-eyed and surprised, Emily responded, "No. Why?"

Valerie emptied the contents of her bag onto the kitchen table. "It's gone!" she exclaimed, looking at her daughter with disappointment. "Are you sure you didn't give in to temptation and eat it?"

A humiliated tear welled up in Emily's eye at the accusation. "No," she said in a trembling voice. "I swear."

"Well, whether you took it or not, the fact remains that there's no chocolate bar to eat anymore," Valerie concluded as she neatly repacked her purse.

Emily returned to her room, bewildered and frustrated. She couldn't explain the disappearance of the chocolate bar. She was certain she hadn't taken it, but the worst part for her was the fear that her mother didn't believe her.

A few moments later, Emily heard her mother talking on the phone again. Valerie spoke in a hushed tone, but Emily clearly heard what she was saying. She slowly descended the stairs to the last step to better eavesdrop.

"I don't know what to do, Anna," Valerie was saying in a frustrated tone. "Now it's all on my shoulders, and not just that. Emily's been acting odd. Of course, she's sad that Albert has left us high and dry, but it's more than just that."

There were a few seconds of silence.

"And strange things are happening," Valerie went on. "Maybe it's nothing."

Another long silence passed. Emily remained still, listening intently without making a sound.

"Things are starting to disappear," Valerie continued. "First a doll, then Emily's hairbrush the other day, and today, even a silly chocolate bar. I'm sure it was in my purse, and now it's gone. Emily swears she didn't touch it. I don't know. Maybe I'm being paranoid, but I have a nagging feeling that Emily is taking things and hiding them. I can't see any other explanation. But why?"

Another silence.

"Anyway, I must go. I'll call you in the next few days. . . . Yes, you too. Take care."

As her mother hang up the receiver, Emily descended the final step and entered the kitchen. "Who was that on the phone?"

"Aunt Anna," Valerie replied.

"How is she?" Emily asked.

"She seems to be doing well."

Emily frowned. "Why has Aunt Anna never come to visit us?"

Valerie's lip quivered. "Your aunt lives *very* far away. Too far."

"Is she older or younger than you?" Emily asked, suddenly curious.

"Younger. By a few seconds," Valerie answered.

Emily looked puzzled. "What does 'by a few seconds' mean?"

"It means we're twins. Born on the same day. It's when a mom carries two babies in her belly instead of one."

Emily's eyes widened in fascination and surprise. "You mean a mom can choose how many babies to have in her belly?"

Valerie laughed. "No, honey. A mom can't choose. It just happens. There are even moms who carry *eight* babies in their belly. God decides these things," Valerie concluded, caressing her daughter's head.

"Will I ever get to meet Aunt Anna?" she asked.

Valerie's expression saddened. "I don't know. Someday, perhaps."

"Is she as beautiful as you?"

Valerie cracked a smile. "She looks just like me."

Emily's eyes widened again. "Really?" she exclaimed. "When I get to meet her, it'll be like having two moms!"

Valerie's smile broadened. "Yes, honey. It'll be like having two moms."

It occurred to Emily then that having two mothers might make up for not having a father around, and the idea of it lifted her spirits a little.

Chapter 3

The next few weeks passed without anything significant going missing. Emily's mother's calls to Aunt Anna sounded mostly happy whenever Emily eavesdropped, which she did often.

Each morning, Emily crossed the day off the 2001 calendar hanging on the refrigerator, silently telling herself that one more day had passed without her father in it. It had been nearly three weeks since he had left. He hadn't returned for his truck, but Emily still had not given up hope.

That morning, she was one box away from the red smiley face her father had drawn on the August 28 box: her first day of school—a day for which she was both excited and nervous.

The little girl imagined that all the parents, mothers *and* fathers, would accompany the kids to school that first day for that big milestone in their child's journey. Emily prayed that her father would be there waiting for her in front of the school when she arrived with her mother. Surely, he wouldn't want to miss her first steps into the new school year. She and her father had talked about the first day of first grade many times during that summer, and he'd told her how proud he was of his "little pearl" and how eager he was to see her walk through the door of the school with her head held high, brave, enthusiastic, and ready to set out on a new path.

Her father had read to her every evening before bed that summer, even challenging her to sound out some of the more difficult words. Now she went to bed alone; her father was no longer there to tuck her in, and her mother was usually too preoccupied with the soap operas she'd recorded during the workday to spend those bedtime moments with her.

Emily turned off the small lamp on her bedside table, laid back, and closed her eyes. She whispered a prayer to God for her father's return. She prayed to see him standing in front of the school, waiting to welcome her with open arms. She would run to him. She would hold him tight. She would plead with him never to leave her again. And he would promise to be with her always. Within a few minutes, Emily fell asleep, dreaming and smiling.

* * *

The following morning was hot and humid. Emily woke up and hurried down to the kitchen. She sat at the table where her mother had prepared a special breakfast of chocolate chip pancakes with homemade whip cream for her first day of school.

"Good morning," Emily murmured sourly.

"Good morning, my little flower," her mother replied, seeming more cheerful than usual.

Emily could not muster a smile in response. Despite her prayers and her vivid imagination, she felt sick at the thought that her father wouldn't be at the school that morning. She was having difficulty holding on to what little hope remained. Silence fell between mother and daughter, awkward and sad.

"Are you ready for this new adventure?" Valerie asked after a few minutes.

Emily nodded, not looking up from her pancakes.

Valerie sighed deeply. "I thought that after school, to celebrate your first day, we could go get ice cream. What do you say?"

Emily nodded again, this time with even less enthusiasm.

Valerie sighed again, then tapped Emily's shoulder and pointed to the clock on the kitchen wall. "Well, I think it's time to get ready. You'll make lots of new friends and learn lots of interesting stuff. And think, perhaps, who knows, they might even teach you to use a microscope!"

At this, Emily felt her first flicker of excitement. *The microscope!*

The great passion of Emily's short life had been discovering that small things were made up of even smaller things. When she turned five, her father had given her a magnifying glass, and with that, Emily had observed virtually everything. She would sit on the steps outside their house and watch ants and other insects go about their daily lives. She knew that there was much more to discover, much more than she could see with the naked eye. On the Fourth of July, Emily had asked her father if she could get a microscope, and he had promised her that if she did well those first few months of first grade, she could ask for a microscope in a letter to Santa Claus. There was a strong possibility that Santa would grant her wish. "Santa Claus *always* rewards good children," her father had told her.

Emily hadn't forgotten. She would do well in class, write her letter, and under the Christmas tree, she was sure she would find that microscope on Christmas morning. That thought filled Emily with energy. She rushed upstairs to get ready for the day. Once dressed, she smiled at herself in the mirror. She felt positive.

Everything will be okay, she tried to convince herself. *He's going to be there.*

* * *

It was nearly eight o'clock when Valerie and Emily set off for Butler Elementary School, which was just under a half mile from their home. For the first day, they had chosen not to use the school bus; like many parents, Emily's mother wanted to say goodbye to her in front of the school on that day of separation and new beginnings. It was also an opportunity to take photos and briefly get to know the teachers and other parents.

Dressed in the pink dress that her father had liked so much, Emily skipped happily, holding her mother's hand. But the closer they got to the school, the more impatient and nervous Emily became. She scrutinized everyone in the area, still hoping to catch a glimpse of her father.

Groups of parents and children were scattered around the parking lot in front of the school. Emily looked around again. Children hugged their parents, saying goodbye before running inside through the glass doors. Fathers and mothers approached, holding their smiling, carefree children's hands. Grandparents took photos and teachers warmly welcomed families in front of the entrance.

But there was no sign of Emily's father.

"It's time to go in," Valerie told her, adjusting the small, flowery backpack on Emily's shoulders. "Don't worry. Everything will be fine. You'll enjoy it, and I'll be out here waiting for you later."

"Just a few more minutes," Emily pleaded, scanning the area again, searching for that face.

Valerie sighed, and Emily flinched. She glanced up at her mother, who watched the goings-on in the parking lot with a pained, hopeless expression. Emily knew then that her father would not come to see her. The reality struck her, crushing her heart past the point of tears. Her father was no longer part of their lives.

"Emily, honey, it's time to go in," her mother insisted, just as the school bell rang.

Emily's shoulder drooped. "Okay," she murmured.

"It's going to be a great adventure," Valerie coached. "You'll like school, and you'll make many new friends. You'll see."

Emily said nothing, shuffling off toward the entrance.

"Remember, I'll be here to pick you up at the end of the day!" her mother shouted as Emily went through the glass door.

Emily pushed away the lingering thoughts of her father's absence and put on a brave face and held her head high. She mustered up enthusiasm for whatever the day ahead had in store.

Chapter 4

Valerie stared forlornly at the door Emily had just disappeared behind. This was the first time Emily would be away from her since Albert had left. She realized then that this day would be tough for her, too. Hoping for Albert's arrival had been hopeless—of this, Valerie was utterly certain.

As the parking lot emptied, she turned and walked back home. She had a lot of work to finish and a delivery to be made before the end of the day. Once home, she got down to work right away. She caught herself frequently staring at the clock over the next couple of hours. Time seemed to crawl, and she was becoming impatient to pick up her daughter from school, to find out how she was, how she had adjusted to the new environment, and how the teacher and the other children had treated her.

"And it's only the first day of school," she whispered as she fed a piece of fabric into the sewing machine.

* * *

Emily's first week of school passed in the blink of an eye. She seemed to have adapted to her new routine rather quickly and talked enthusiastically about the new friends she'd made. At two in the afternoon, as she did every day, Valerie stood by the fence, anxiously waiting for the yellow bus on which Emily would return home.

When it arrived, Emily descended, smiling, turned toward the bus, and waved to her friends. Valerie crouched down to hug her daughter, but Emily's gaze was fixated on her friends, who were waving back through the windows. She didn't look at her mother until the bus disappeared around the corner.

"How was your day, honey?" Valerie asked with a tight smile, as she took a drag from her cigarette.

"I had so much fun," Emily replied.

"Did you learn something new?" Valerie asked, swallowing down unusual pangs of jealousy.

"A lot!" the child said with excitement as she ran toward the house.

Valerie watched Emily from behind, realizing how much her daughter had changed in just one short week. She had not seen Emily this happy and radiant since Albert's unceremonious departure. She felt her heart squeeze and followed her "little flower" into the house.

Once inside, Valerie sat at the kitchen table, where Emily was already seated, munching on one of the homemade cookies Valerie had left out for her. She smiled to see her enjoying it so much, especially because she'd taken time away from her sewing to make them.

"Your birthday is just three short days away," Valerie remarked. "How would you like to celebrate?"

"Can I invite some friends over for a party?" Emily asked with a mouthful of wet cookie crumbs.

"Sure, that would be fun," Valerie said after a brief thoughtful pause. She decided it would be a good idea for her to get to know Emily's new friends. "Would you like me to make you a yummy chocolate cake with princess sprinkles on top?"

Emily nodded vigorously as she finished the last cookie on the plate.

"Very well, then, a chocolate cake it is!" Valerie concluded, affectionately ruffling Emily's hair.

* * *

When she wasn't working or watching her soaps, Valerie spent the next three days organizing and preparing for Emily's party. She had contacted the mothers of Emily's five "best" friends, and they had all eagerly accepted the invitation. The party was scheduled for 3 p.m., right after school, on September 10, Emily's sixth birthday—the first birthday she would spend without Albert.

When Emily returned home from school, the living room was all set for the party. Valerie had hung balloons all around the room and laid out a colorful tablecloth spread with bowls of snacks and cookies on the coffee table. The birthday cake was in the fridge, ready to be cut.

Emily's friends arrived on time, each handing Emily a small, gift-wrapped, beribboned present. Following Valerie's instructions, Emily placed them all in a corner near the entrance, at the foot of the stairs, leading to the second floor. For over two hours, the girls played, colored, and enjoyed the snacks Valerie had arranged on the table.

When it was time to cut the cake, Valerie closed the curtain in the living room to darken the room, lit the candles, and presented the cake, leading the party in singing the birthday song. Emily looked ecstatic as she closed her eyes, made her wish, and blew out the candles with a single breath. All her friends applauded, and Valerie served each one a slice of cake and a glass of apple juice.

At the end of the party, the mothers arrived to pick up their daughters. Valerie watched as, one by one, they hugged and said goodbye to Emily at the door and put on their jackets. The mothers seemed nice enough to Valerie, and their little girls looked like miniature replicas of them with their perfect brown curls and blond ponytails and their expensive clothing.

Once the last guest departed, Valerie went into the kitchen to tidy up, while Emily went to her room to change out of her party dress. Thirty minutes later, Emily rushed back downstairs and into the kitchen, where her mother was still busy washing dishes.

"Can I open my presents now?" she asked.

"Of course, honey," Valerie replied with a smile.

Emily scampered out of the room with palpable excitement. For an instant, there was silence, and then Emily shouted from the living room, "Mom!"

Valerie dried her hands on her apron and hurried into the other room. "What's wrong?"

Emily stood at the foot of the stairs, swinging her head in confusion. "My presents," she said, her voice trembling. "They're gone. I can't find them. They were here!"

Valerie looked around the room with an equally perplexed expression. "They're gone?" she asked, her voice filled with confusion.

"I don't know!" Emily cried. "I don't know!"

They searched everywhere, checked under every piece of furniture, behind every door, and inside every closet. Tears filled Emily's eyes as Valerie repeated her same, frantic efforts.

Valerie watched her little girl dart back and forth through the house, her eyes wide with shock and terror. She knew all too well what this meant–another disappearance. Weeks had passed without any incidents. All Emily's presents had seemingly vanished into thin air.

Valerie eventually halted Emily's frenetic rush, placing her hands on the child's shoulders and locking eyes with her. "Are you absolutely sure you didn't take them and put them somewhere and then forget?"

"I'm sure!" Emily replied with desperation. Her voice rose to a scream. "I'm sure!" She covered her face with her hands.

Valerie hugged her tightly, trying to provide comfort. "We'll figure this out," she said with determination. "I promise."

Emily let her arms fall to her sides, a gesture of exhaustion, defeat, and utter distress.

"We'll figure this out," Valerie repeated.

* * *

Emily spent the rest of the afternoon in her room, crying into her pillow. It wasn't until dinnertime that she finally decided to come downstairs.

However, halfway down the staircase, she heard her mother on the phone again. She stopped to listen, her curiosity piqued as usual. She was talking to Aunt Anna again. As far as Emily knew, Aunt Anna was the only one she ever spoke to, outside of clients who needed something tailored or created.

"No one else was here. I watched all the guests leave, and the presents were right where I told Emily to leave them."

Emily stopped at the foot of the stairs.

"She doesn't remember taking them. She says they disappeared into thin air."

Emily's chest tightened in shame.

"I'm worried. Why would Emily hide her presents? And where? We've searched everywhere. She certainly didn't have time to bury them in the garden! There's something very wrong."

Silence. Emily lowered her head, feeling miserable. Her mother didn't believe her. *But if it was me,* she thought, *where did I put the presents? And why can't I remember?* That thought filled her eyes with tears once again.

"Let's talk later. I have to get dinner ready," Valerie concluded.

Emily heard the phone rattle into the cradle and moved to the kitchen doorway. Valerie turned as she entered, and her eyes widened.

"Are you crying again?" her mother asked, clearly dismayed.

"Mom, it wasn't me who made the presents disappear. I swear!" Emily said, sobbing.

Valerie approached her daughter and hugged her without responding. All the tears of sorrow, disappointment, and confusion she'd bottled in the past few weeks poured out of Emily, and her mother held her as she wept. After a few minutes, Emily raised her head to see her mother wiping tears from her eyes.

"Let's not think about it for now," Valerie suggested. "There has to be an explanation for these strange disappearances. Don't give up hope; sooner or later, those presents will reappear, and you can play with them. Don't worry. I'll take care of you, honey."

The ring of the phone pierced the moment of sadness and comfort between mother and daughter. Valerie pulled away from the little one's arms and went to answer it. "Hello?"

Emily thought she heard her father's name, spoken by a female voice from the other end, before her mother hung up without responding.

"Who was it, Mom?" Emily asked, confused by the strange reaction.

"No one, honey," Valerie replied, reaching for her pack of cigarettes. "Someone just dialed the wrong number."

* * *

Several days after her party, Emily's presents still had not surfaced, and her hairband and her beloved magnifying glass had also gone missing. Emily had heard her mother on the phone with Aunt Anna a few times about the mysterious and continuous disappearances, and each time, she had raised doubts about Emily's honesty. As always, Emily listened from the bottom of the stairs, confused by her mother's comments.

Emily was certain she hadn't touched those packages and couldn't understand where all the other items had gone, or at least, she didn't remember what she had done with them. Doubt grew within her. She wondered how it could be possible, where she had hidden everything, and most importantly, why she didn't remember doing it. Was it some sort of magic?

These thoughts began to deeply disturb her. But her happy island, the place where she felt normal, was at school, with her friends. She eagerly went to class every day. She enjoyed learning new things and adored her teacher. Every morning, she ran eagerly to catch the school bus, and every afternoon, she returned home, where Valerie was always waiting for her, standing by the wooden fence.

* * *

On the morning of September 17, Emily missed the school bus, and Valerie had to walk her to school. Breakfast wasn't ready for her as it usually was when she'd gotten to the kitchen that morning. Valerie told her not to rush when she placed a dish of scrambled eggs and a piece of buttered toast in front of her. Emily had just taken a bite of her toast when she heard the bus pull up. She'd rushed to the window with her mouth still full, but the bus had already closed its doors and started driving away.

"Mom! My bus! It left me!" the little girl shouted.

Valerie ran to the window and let out a frustrated sigh. "Don't worry, honey. I'll walk you there," she said, with a comforting hand on her daughter's shoulders.

Emily let her arms fall to her sides. "I know. But I like taking the bus. All my friends are on it." With slumped shoulders, she returned to the kitchen table.

"I understand," her mother said soothingly. "But I have something that will make you happy today." She headed to her workroom and reappeared a few moments later, holding a small pink windbreaker. "I had planned to give this to you on Sunday for our downtown trip. But since you're feeling sad, you can have it now." She handed the garment to Emily.

Emily gaped in surprise. She grabbed the jacket and put it on. "It fits me perfectly!" she exclaimed as she admired her reflection in the kitchen window.

"Of course!" Valerie replied with amusement. "Your mother knows your size well."

Emily met Valerie's eyes, and they shared a laugh.

On the way to school, Emily practically skipped the entire time. "I can't wait for the girls to see my new windbreaker," she gushed, squeezing her mother's hand. "I'm sure they'll all like it!"

"I'm sure they will, honey," Valerie replied.

"I really, really like school," Emily said, feeling good about the day ahead even though she had missed the bus. "The kids in my class are fun. I like the teacher and what we're learning. Someday, I'm going to be a famous research scientist. They'll call me from all over the world, and with my beautiful microscope, I'll discover lots of stuff."

Valerie smiled down at her, a twinkle of pride in her eyes. "Of course, of course."

Mother and daughter entered the school together and headed for the main office. The other students were already in their classrooms, and the receptionist was not at her station. Valerie looked around, searching for someone to help them. At that moment, a teacher entered.

"May I assist you?" she asked, scrutinizing the pair.

"Yes," Valerie replied, "my daughter, Emily, missed the bus this morning, and I had to walk her here."

"Which class?" the teacher asked.

"Class 101. First grade," Valerie replied.

The teacher looked around, and Emily followed her glance. Still no sign of the receptionist.

"Okay, just for today, you can accompany your daughter to the classroom," the teacher replied, pointing the way. "It's just around the corner. Please leave right after. No one is supposed to be unattended in the halls."

"Mom, I know where my class is," Emily said hastily, then turned and briskly walked off on her own down the hallway. Her mother gave a resigned sigh, and her footsteps hurried to catch up.

The corridors were empty. All the children were in class for that first hour, and the silence was broken only by the distant chatter or singing of the students. The walls were peppered with drawings, and in one corner, a display case proudly showcased the small trophies students had won in various competitions and sports activities.

Once they reached the classroom, Emily took off her windbreaker and hung it on the coatrack outside the door, next to those of her classmates. She paused for a few seconds, admiring it one last time. Then she glanced at her classmates' jackets and smiled. Two other jackets were pink like hers. Emily stopped to observe them and then looked back at hers.

She turned to see her mother watching the scene with amusement, and then mother and daughter parted ways.

When snack time arrived, Emily and her classmates filed into the hallway to make their way to the schoolyard, where they would eat and play for a half hour. Emily was near the back of the line, and by the time she emerged, the line had dissolved into a confused, chattering crowd in front of the coatrack.

Two of the jackets, the two pink ones like Emily's, were in tatters—and pieces of cloth lay on the floor.

The teacher looked around, her expression bewildered. "Who could have done this?" she asked noone in particular.

Emily looked at her classmates' surprised, stricken faces. Then she turned to the coatrack. *Her* pink jacket was intact, still hanging. She couldn't imagine how she had done such a thing to the other pink jackets, but she felt the heat of responsibility rise to her face just the same.

* * *

Valerie was sitting at her work desk when the phone on the kitchen wall rang. She glanced at the clock, then headed to the kitchen and lifted the receiver. "Hello!" she answered, determined.

"Good morning," said a female voice. "I'm Mrs. Blair, the secretary of the Butler Elementary School principal. May I speak to Mrs. Barton?"

Valerie frowned. "Yes, this is she."

"Mrs. Barton," said Mrs. Blair brusquely, "it would be best if you came to the school immediately. The principal would like to see you as soon as possible."

"Has something happened to Emily?" Valerie asked, anxious.

There were a few seconds of silence.

"No, Mrs. Barton. Emily is fine. But please come as soon as possible."

"Of course! Right away!" Valerie replied.

The call abruptly disconnected without a farewell. Valerie returned to her workroom, grabbed her jacket, rushed out of the house, and practically ran to the school.

It took just over ten minutes to arrive at the building to which she had accompanied her daughter only three hours earlier. She entered the school and found the receptionist and the principal waiting for her in the foyer. Without much small talk, the principal escorted Valerie to her office, motioned for Valerie to take a seat, closed the door, and sat down behind her desk.

The woman, slightly overweight, fixed Valerie with a serious gaze for a few seconds before speaking, "Mrs. Barton, something unpleasant and, I would say, quite startling, happened this morning. We are not only surprised but also deeply saddened by it. I wanted to see you first, not only to prevent any disturbance or painful actions but also, and most importantly, to understand. To understand the reason for what happened."

Valerie stared at the woman with a confused expression while a growing sense of dread for what the principal was about to tell her grew inside her.

"You should know, Mrs. Barton, that for the safety of our students, our school is equipped with closed-circuit cameras. And what we witnessed this morning was not only unprecedented but astonishing. A sad and perplexing event that has left us baffled."

* * *

When Emily returned home from school that day, Valerie wasn't waiting for her with a smile by the fence. She got off the bus and looked around, confused, searching for her mother. She continued on her own toward the front door, entered the house, and found Valerie sitting at the kitchen table, head bowed, in tears.

"What's wrong, Mom?" Emily asked with a trembling voice. She felt a growing sense of terror inside her. The fear that what had happened at school that day was her responsibility froze her in front of her devastated mother.

"I don't remember anything, Mom, I swear," Emily said without waiting for her mother's response, hoping to receive a comforting look.

Valerie slowly turned her gaze to the child. Her eyes were red and swollen. Her look was sad. Resigned. "It's okay," her mother whispered, struggling to muster a smile.

Emily embraced her mother and burst into convulsive tears. Valerie silently stroked her head as she released her emotions.

"Sit down, honey," Valerie instructed after a few minutes. "We need to talk about something important."

Emily obeyed and sat at the kitchen table, tears still stinging her eyes.

"For a while, you'll need to stay home and not go to school," Valerie began.

Emily's eyes widened.

"Just for a little while," Valerie added hastily. "Just long enough to figure out what's going on with you. I'll try to find someone to teach you here."

Emily couldn't believe what she was hearing. She wouldn't be going to school? She wouldn't see or play with her friends?

"I've called a special doctor," her mother continued. "She wants to have a chat with you. We have an appointment in a couple of days."

Emily couldn't breathe.

Her mother reached out and cupped Emily's face in her shaking hands. Tears rolled down her face again. "No one will do anything bad to you," she whispered. "I'll protect you."

Emily staggered out of her chair, ran up to her bedroom, and slammed the door. She collapsed onto her bed and burst into tears once again, feeling completely dejected.

* * *

Emily and her mother didn't talk much about what had happened in the days that followed. Valerie divided her time between her sewing work and working with Emily on schoolwork. Whenever they worked on Emily's lessons, Valerie wore a positive, happy face, trying to be both friend and teacher to her daughter. But Emily was sad. She often found herself staring out of the window, lost in her thoughts and wondering why this was happening to her.

On the afternoon of September 25, a week after Emily had stopped going to school, Valerie put on her jacket and applied some makeup. "I need to go downtown to buy some fabric," she told Emily as she fixed her hair in front of the bathroom mirror. "You can't come. I have to be quick. I have a delivery tomorrow, and I just realized I don't have enough fabric."

"But I really wanted an ice cream," Emily replied, disappointed.

"I know," her mother said gently. "I promise we'll go together on Saturday, and you can have your ice cream. Okay?" She kissed Emily's head. "And don't open the door for anyone while I'm out," she added as she was already at the door, about to leave.

"Okay," Emily replied and got back to her schoolwork.

Valerie left the house, and Emily found herself alone in the silence. She rushed to the window and watched her mother hurrying away until she disappeared around the corner, out of sight. She wasn't happy about being left alone.

The ringing of the telephone shattered the silence. Emily jumped in surprise, then rushed to the kitchen to pick up the receiver.

"Hello, Barton residence," she said, as seriously as she could. "Who's calling?"

"Hello, may I speak with Albert Barton, please?" the female voice on the other end inquired.

"My father is not here," Emily replied.

"Can I leave him a message? You must be little Emily, right? I'm Attorney David Coleman's assistant."

"Yes, I'm Emily," she responded, feeling her serious façade waver. "But my father is gone. Forever. My mother says he's not coming back."

"What does *not coming back* mean?" the assistant asked, sounding confused.

Emily wondered why that wasn't clear to the lady but explained anyway, "One morning, I woke up, and he was gone. He left a letter for Mom and went away."

There were a few seconds of silence.

"And he never came back?" the woman asked. "Never? Not even to see you?"

"No, ma'am. Never. It's been more than a month," Emily replied, her voice trembling.

There was silence again.

"Is your mom at home?"

"No, ma'am. She went downtown to buy some fabric. But she said she'd be back soon."

"Emily, can you tell your mom to call me?" the woman asked. "Can you write? If I give you a phone number, can you write it down?"

"Yes. Wait, let me get my pencil," the child replied with the enthusiasm of someone on an important mission. She retrieved a pencil from her mother's desk and returned to the phone. "I'm ready!" the girl said, determined.

The lawyer's assistant dictated the number. She had Emily repeat it to make sure she had written it correctly, and then she gave her both her name and the lawyer's name.

"It's very important that your mom calls me, Emily," the woman insisted. "Don't forget to give her the message when she returns."

"Of course, ma'am."

"And remember one thing, Emily. Your father loves you very much. He told me that, so don't doubt it." The woman ended the call.

Emily's heart lit up upon hearing those words. Her father loved her; the woman had confirmed it. She knew it was true, even though she couldn't explain why her father hadn't come to see her in all this time.

Chapter 5

When Valerie returned home shortly after, Emily rushed to the door with a note in her hand.

"Mom, Mom, a lady called!" Emily practically shouted. Her eyes were bright with excitement. "She said she's a lawyer's assistant. She was looking for Dad! She left her number for you. She said you should call her as soon as possible! Maybe she knows where Dad is!"

Valerie stared first at Emily, then at the small note written in pencil. She grabbed it from Emily's hand and, without responding, placed the fabric she was holding on the kitchen table. She stared at the note again with a heavy heart. "What did you tell this lady?" she asked without taking her eyes off the paper.

"She asked if she could talk to Dad," Emily replied in an almost military tone. "I told her he had gone away, and then she asked to speak to you. But you weren't here, so she told me to tell you to call her. She said it's important, Mom."

Valerie remained silent for a few seconds. She turned to the child and smiled at her. "Honey, why don't you go play in the yard while I make this call?"

"Okay," said Emily, turning and bouncing toward the front door.

Once alone, Valerie dialed the number, steeling herself in the few seconds it took for the assistant to answer, "Law office of David Coleman. How may I assist?"

Valerie glanced toward the front door to make sure Emily couldn't overhear the conversation. "This is Valerie Barton."

* * *

Emily sat on the steps in front of the house. She had no toys; in the few weeks since her birthday, the few things she'd had slowly disappeared, one after the other. After Charlie, her Barbie with the broken arm had vanished, and even her lucky ceramic turtle had disappeared.

So she found herself forced to play with a couple of rocks from the garden, one small stone the size of her palm and the other a bit larger. She imagined that the small one was her, and the larger one was her father. She made them hop, side by side, as if impersonating the two of them walking together. She rehearsed the scene of her father's hoped-for arrival home: She would jump for joy, they would hug, and they would walk along a path, talking about the journey her father had taken during that time, about adventures in extraordinary and wild places too remote for him to call or come back to her.

Emily immersed herself so deeply in that imaginary world that she could almost see the scene. She smiled with the first genuine happiness she'd felt in a week. She played the game with enthusiasm, savoring the pleasant feeling it gave her for a time.

Over ten minutes had passed when her mother appeared at the door.

"Honey," she said with a shaky voice, "go take a shower and get ready for dinner."

Emily looked up and studied her mother. She knew that expression very well; her mother was not happy. That phone call hadn't gone well, and something had disturbed her. So Emily avoided asking what the lady had to say about her father. Instead, she got up and went upstairs, as her mother had instructed.

* * *

The following Monday morning, October 1, marked Emily's first visit with the "special" doctor Valerie had contacted. To get there, however, they had to drive, so they took Albert's truck. This was the first time it had been driven since the day Albert had taken Emily dress shopping at the old Mystic Mall.

"How far away is the doctor's office?" Emily asked as she buckled herself into the backseat.

"It's not a long ride, just ten miles," her mother replied, glancing at Emily in the rearview mirror. "It's in New London. A small town nearby."

Valerie backed the truck out of the garage very slowly. She had never driven much; she'd never needed to. She had grown up in a place where everything she needed was within walking distance. Besides, Albert had done most of the driving once they'd gotten married.

Fifteen minutes later, they reached the center of the town. It was half past eleven when she parked on Chicago Avenue, a short walk from the clinic.

Valerie took Emily by the hand and led her to the facility in silence. Waiting for them would be Dr. Taylor Jackson, a child psychiatrist with whom Valerie had previously discussed Emily's issues. The fifty-year-old doctor had twenty-two years of experience in the field, and she had shown great interest in Emily's case.

Once in the clinic, a petite woman with dark brown eyes and a friendly smile greeted them from behind the reception desk. “Good morning. Do you have an appointment?” she asked politely.

“Yes, with Dr. Jackson,” Valerie replied.

The receptionist smiled again, and as she grabbed the phone, she looked over at Emily and nodded toward a bowl of lollipops resting between them on the counter.

The girl’s face lit up as she immediately plucked a strawberry-flavored one. Valerie smiled indulgently.

“While I advise the doctor,” the woman said, nodding to a glass-walled room on their left, “you can sit in the waiting room.”

Mother and daughter sat side by side in the otherwise empty room. About ten minutes later, Dr. Jackson appeared at the door. She was tall and dark skinned, with long black hair tied at the nape of her neck.

“Good morning!” the doctor said, smiling at the child. “You must be Emily.”

Hearing her name, Emily jumped to her feet. “Yes, that’s me!” she eagerly replied.

“Nice to meet you,” the doctor said. “I’d like to talk to your mom for a few minutes first, if that’s okay with you.”

Emily nodded and sat back down.

“Mrs. Sonny will bring you some crayons and paper while you wait,” Dr. Jackson said, gesturing toward the receptionist. “Is that okay?”

Emily smiled again. “Yes, thank you!” she said as the receptionist approached with a box of crayons and a drawing pad.

Meanwhile, Valerie followed the doctor down the hallway to her office. Dr. Jackson sat in one of two chairs separated by a small coffee table and gestured for Valerie to sit in the other, and then she studied Valerie for a few seconds.

"So, Mrs. Barton," the doctor began, opening her notebook, "tell me about these disappearances. When did they start, and how does Emily behave about them?"

Valerie lowered her gaze to her clasped hands and sighed. "About a month and a half ago, my husband, Emily's father, left us, leaving only a farewell letter. I believe it was the day after that things started to disappear. At first, small things. A doll. A hairbrush. Small toys. All very strange, but I didn't worry too much at first. Like Emily, I was confused about why and how all of this was happening."

"All the things that went missing belonged to Emily?" Dr. Jackson asked without taking her eyes off her notebook.

"Yes, everything was hers," Valerie confirmed. "Her favorite doll, Charlie. The brush she uses before going to bed. Her magnifying glass. Emily has a passion for chemistry, and she loved that magnifying glass. And many other small things. But then . . ." Valerie paused.

"Then?" Dr. Jackson pressed with a curious look.

"Then," Valerie nearly whispered, "on her birthday, after the party with her classmates, all the gifts she'd received disappeared into thin air."

Dr. Jackson stopped writing and stared at Valerie, her expression incredulous. "What do you mean? Disappeared into thin air?"

"Well, five gifts, still wrapped, were all neatly arranged at the entrance. After the party, while I was cleaning up the kitchen, I heard Emily scream, so I rushed to see why. The gifts were gone. We've searched everywhere but haven't found them." Valerie lowered her gaze to the table.

There were a few seconds of silence. Dr. Jackson took a deep breath, scribbling her notes, and raised her gaze to Valerie again. "How did Emily react?"

"She was devastated," Valerie said sadly. "As I told you, we searched everywhere. Nothing. Emily swears she was upstairs changing clothes while I was in the kitchen tidying up after the party. No one else was in the house."

Jackson's expression was intrigued. "You have no idea where she might hide or dispose of all these things? We're talking about some rather bulky items. They certainly didn't just disappear."

Valerie shook her head. "None. I thought she might've buried them in the garden, but clearly, she wouldn't have had the time or strength for that. I know it sounds strange. But in that moment, you consider anything. Even though . . ."

"Even though what, Mrs. Barton?" Jackson pressed.

"Behind our house, there's a small slope that leads down to the river. It's the only place I can imagine, but I don't know how she could manage to get out, dispose of everything there, and come back home without my noticing. But really, I have no other explanation. I suppose I *was* in the kitchen for quite some time. The gifts are simply not in the house."

Dr. Jackson tapped her pencil on her notepad. Valerie waited anxiously, wondering what the doctor would say. She knew there were many places in a house where something could be hidden. She remembered that as a child, she'd hidden her sweets under a loose floorboard in the parquet flooring. Would Dr. Jackson chalk up Emily's missing things to something like this?

"Have you asked Emily what she remembers from that moment?" Jackson asked then.

Valerie suppressed a sigh of relief, staring at a tiny water stain on the table in front of her. "Yes. She says she was upstairs. She was crying desperately when we talked about it. Just like with all the other things, she claims not to remember touching them, moving them, or hiding them." A tear stung her eye and streaked down her face. "A mystery, Doctor. It's really as if everything literally vanished into thin air. And then, the incident at school that I told you about over the phone was what brought me to you . . ."

"A mystery," the doctor agreed solemnly, her gaze fixed on Valerie. "Yes. It does seem like a mystery. But perhaps behind this mystery, there's something bigger. Something deeper. If Emily throws away, destroys, or hides things she cares about and claims not to remember doing it, I have only one explanation that comes to mind at the moment. But let me speak with her first."

* * *

Emily was engrossed in coloring in the picture she'd drawn of a house and a yard under the watchful eye of Mrs. Sonny when she heard her mother and Dr. Jackson return to the waiting area. Emily carried on, completely absorbed in adding detail: a girl chasing a butterfly.

"Emily," Dr. Jackson said after a moment, "are you ready to talk with me?"

The child raised her head, smiling. "Yes, that's why I'm here, right?"

The four shared a laugh, and then Dr. Jackson took Emily by the hand and led her into her office. Once inside, Emily sat on the couch, and the doctor sat beside her.

Emily sighed as she looked around the room with curiosity.

"Are you nervous?" the doctor asked with kindness.

"No," Emily replied. "Maybe a little. I don't know."

Dr. Jackson smiled. "You have no reason to be. We're here just to have a chat."

Emily nodded. "I know. That's what Mom told me. A special doctor to talk to. No shots or yucky syrups."

"Exactly!" Dr. Jackson exclaimed, laughing once more. There were then a few seconds of silence. "So, Emily, what do you like most about school?"

Emily thought a moment before answering, "I like a lot of things. My friends, the teacher, learning new things."

Dr. Jackson continued to ask questions about school, as well as Emily's food preferences and various topics. They talked extensively about her passion for microscopes and discovering the worlds within tiny things and her curiosity about the subject. Emily knew exactly what she wanted to do when she grew up: she would become a laboratory researcher.

Emily's shyness slowly melted away, and just as it did so, Dr. Jackson's questions changed. "I imagine you miss your father very much," she said.

Emily felt a pinch in the center of her chest, and she paused, dropping her chin. "Yes," she whispered, "very much . . ."

"What did you think when you found out your father had left?" Dr. Jackson asked gently.

Another silent pause.

"I thought he would come back," Emily admitted. "Sooner or later."

"You don't think that anymore?"

Emily shook her head. "I still think it. But I'm starting to not believe it anymore."

"Why don't you believe it anymore?" Dr. Jackson sounded sad.

"Because he would have come back for my first day of school," Emily reasoned. "Or for my birthday. And he didn't."

The doctor paused. In the few intervening seconds of silence, Emily felt her eyes begin to sting. She had never admitted this before, that she'd started to believe her father might never come back. It hurt her deeply to confess this, even to an understanding adult like Dr. Jackson.

"Who is Charlie, Emily?" the doctor asked calmly.

Emily felt her shoulders droop. "Charlie was my favorite doll," Emily replied, almost whispering. Her sadness grew sharper.

" *Was*? Why was that?" Jackson asked again.

Emily's heart started to pound. "Because he disappeared. One day I woke up, and he wasn't on the chair where I had left him."

"What do you think happened to him?" the doctor asked.

Emily thought for a few seconds, but no answers came to mind. She grimaced in frustration. "I don't know," she said with a shrug. "It's gone. Maybe someone took him, I don't know."

Dr. Jackson sighed, made a note in her notebook, and then continued to ask questions. Some were about the disappearances, others about Emily's life. She prompted Emily to analyze and verify her memory on various topics, from simple mathematics to recent events to others that were less recent. Emily was exhausted after more than an hour of questions, and she was relieved when Dr. Jackson decided to conclude it for the time being.

* * *

Between what Emily and Valerie had told her about what had been happening in recent weeks, it was difficult for Dr. Jackson to form a clear picture of what was happening to the child. However, she had some hypotheses and needed to discuss them with Emily's mother.

Once Emily was once again seated in the waiting room, Dr. Jackson called Valerie into her office. They sat as before, facing each other.

Under the weight of Mrs. Barton's intent stare, Dr. Jackson consulted her notes for a few moments before saying, "So, Mrs. Barton, I must say that Emily is very sweet and, most importantly, very intelligent. As you had mentioned to me before, she has no recollection or explanation of where all the disappeared items ended up. And I believe her. She *truly* doesn't remember, and my various attempts to stimulate her memory have not yielded any results that would suggest or imply a neurological problem. Nothing."

Valerie's expression was worried. "So, what's happening, Doctor?"

Dr. Jackson cleared her throat. "I have a hypothesis, but it's a tentative one. It's the first thing that came to mind after listening to both of you." She paused for a few seconds, fixing her gaze on Valerie. "I believe it might be a peculiar form of kleptomania. Commonly, kleptomania is an impulse control disorder where a person steals things because they can't control the desire for possession, regardless of whether the item is useful. In Emily's case, her sudden abandonment by her father may have triggered a different response in her mind. Emily's response is distinct from conventional kleptomania—she believes that everything she cares about will eventually vanish, and in her mind, she makes it happen unknowingly. It's a preliminary hypothesis, but the fact that these events started immediately after her father's abandonment reminds me of a very similar situation with another patient I helped years ago. The only difference—and this is why I want to do further research, as well as speak with Emily some more—is the absence of memory of the act. Her kleptomania is likely accompanied by a form of dissociative amnesia."

"I don't understand. What does that mean?" Valerie asked, her voice breaking from the tension.

"In my career, I've dealt with many cases of dissociative amnesia. It often occurs in children who have experienced severe trauma. In Emily's case, the responsible trauma is her father's abandonment. However, it's rare to encounter patients suffering from kleptomania, especially at such a young age. Moreover, I've never encountered a case of kleptomania associated with dissociative amnesia. If that's what it is—based on what you've told me and what I've gathered from speaking with her—Emily steals items that have sentimental value to her and somehow disposes of them. Then she forgets she's done it."

Valerie lowered her head. "And what can be done to help her recover? Is there a cure?" she asked without raising her gaze.

"Of course," Dr Jackson answered readily. "The timelines can be uncertain in cases like these, but both dissociative amnesia and kleptomania can be treated. Emily is still very young, which makes the process easier. However, we need to be certain that this is the issue. As I said, this is just a hypothesis. I'd like to consult with some colleagues, especially with an old professor of mine who has studied and analyzed many cases of kleptomania." She tapped her pen on her notebook.

Valerie offered a polite smile. "And what should I do in the meantime?" she asked, her voice tinged with concern. "How can I help my daughter?"

Dr. Jackson braced herself for Valerie's response, even as she replied, "In this situation, one thing is certain. Emily's distress is undoubtedly caused by her father's abandonment, especially because he left abruptly without any explanation. It would greatly help her to see him again. Is there any possibility you could somehow locate your husband, Mrs. Barton?"

Valerie's expression became irritated. "Why would I? How would it help Emily to see her father for a few hours? It would just give her false hope. Albert has already hurt her too much!"

"It would help Emily to better understand the situation," Dr. Jackson replied gingerly. "I'm sure the child has many questions for her father. Questions she keeps inside and to which she might only find answers by seeing him again. The awareness that he hasn't disappeared from her life forever might be the best remedy for what's happening in her mind."

Valerie lowered her head once more. "I wouldn't know where to locate him. He left a letter and disappeared. I woke up one morning, and he was gone. He didn't even take his car. He practically vanished into thin air."

"Do you still have the letter, Mrs. Barton? May I read it?" Dr. Jackson asked gently.

Valerie shook her head. "No. I destroyed it shortly after. I was angry."

There were a few seconds of silence. Dr. Jackson made note of Valerie's response and demeanor in her notebook.

"What else do you suggest I do?" Valerie asked. "Do you think it's a good idea for Emily to continue studying from home?"

Dr. Jackson looked into the woman's eyes and took a few seconds to reflect. "I believe it's not advisable to send her back to school. Although I think it's unlikely, going to school might pose a risk to herself and other children. I'll give you the number for the Department of Social Services, who can help you get homeschooling assistance. This is until we know exactly what's going on in Emily's mind. After I've consulted with my colleagues, I'll contact you to schedule our next session."

Valerie nodded. Dr. Jackson closed her notebook, mulling over the fascinating case as she rose to escort Valerie back to the waiting room.

* * *

As Valerie unlocked the truck, Emily asked if she could sit in the front seat. After some hesitation, Valerie agreed, and they climbed aboard. She securely fastened her daughter's seatbelt and gave her a quick smile.

"Can I change the radio station?" Emily asked as Valerie turned the key and the engine rumbled to life.

Valerie gave her daughter a mock disapproving look and then chucked. "Okay, but at a low volume. Alright?"

Valerie backed out of their parking space as Emily switched to a country music station, her father's favorite. Valerie glanced at her daughter as the first notes warbled out of the speakers. Emily looked somber. Valerie knew that she missed her father terribly, and she wondered if Emily was recalling the last time she had been in the car with him. Valerie reached over and lowered the volume, nearly muting John Montgomery's "The Little Girl".

"Did you like Dr. Jackson?" she asked.

"Yes, very much," Emily replied. "She's nice."

"Would you like to meet her again? Another time, I mean?"

Emily was silent for a moment. "Does the special doctor think I'm sick?" Emily asked calmly.

Valerie glanced at her again, then reached over and squeezed her small hand. "No, honey. Dr. Jackson thinks you're a special little girl. That's why she wants to talk to you again."

Emily smiled proudly.

"And she also told me that you're so special that you'll have a special teacher who will come to our house to help you with your lessons for a while."

Emily's expression darkened. "Does that mean I can't go back to school?"

"Just for a little while," Valerie reassured her. "Just for a little while."

For the rest of the ride home, mother and daughter were silent, listening to the radio. Once they arrived home, Valerie returned to her work, and Emily went to play on the steps of the house, arranging the same small stones in the same game Valerie had seen her play many times since her possessions had disappeared.

* * *

In the week that followed, Dr. Jackson contacted the Department of Social Services. They assigned Emily a teacher who came to their home every morning to assist with her schoolwork. Paola Ford was a young psychology graduate of Yale University, but originally, she'd hailed from the nearby town of Groton. She was blond, slim, and short, with a sweet smile. Emily immediately fell in love with her and gushed about her to Dr. Jackson in the second of many weekly sessions.

On the first day, Paola Ford arrived with a small bag of chocolate candies that Emily devoured during her first day of lessons. Valerie shared her disapproval with the doctor; she saw the danger of disappointing the child if that attention wasn't repeated several times in the future, and she worried that Emily's emotional fragility couldn't withstand even small disappointments.

Every morning, from nine o'clock until noon, Ms. Ford followed the official curriculum provided by the State Department of Education. Her job was to prepare Emily for the semester exams. Emily was very intelligent and quickly grasped every lesson; from writing to mathematics, there was no subject in which the girl struggled. Ms. Ford shared her amazement at the child's abilities with Valerie several times, and Valerie passed these sentiments on to Dr. Jackson.

As the weeks went by, Dr. Jackson noted a change in Emily's demeanor. At first, Emily approached their sessions with serenity and enthusiasm, but as the weeks went by, it was clear they had begun to wear on her. The constant questions, which were always the same, the digging into her memory and emotions—Emily couldn't understand the need for these discussions.

After a particularly fruitless session, Dr. Jackson decided to address the issue. "Emily, I get the impression that you don't enjoy talking with me every week anymore."

Emily had been distracted, looking out the window at the tree branches swaying in the strong October wind. She turned her gaze back to the doctor before responding, "I like talking to you. But I still don't understand what my problem is. Why can't I go to school like everyone else? Why don't I have friends anymore? What's wrong with me?"

Dr. Jackson pondered for a moment. During that month, she had consulted with other colleagues about her suspicions regarding Emily's condition. They all agreed that it was a fascinating clinical situation and that the trauma of the child's father's abandonment had caused her strange form of kleptomania and dissociative amnesia. It was the only plausible explanation, according to these doctors.

They had all offered to talk to Emily, but Dr. Jackson had reservations, believing it wasn't the right time. She thought it would be too stressful for the girl. During those weeks, she had mostly tried to stimulate Emily's memory and get her to talk about her father, her relationship with him, and her relationship with Valerie.

One day, Emily had told her she wished to meet her aunt Anna, whom her mother spoke to almost every day on the phone. Her mother had explained to Emily that her aunt lived far away, and she didn't know when they would be able to meet.

Dr. Jackson noticed, in that story and in many other moments, that Emily needed more than just her mother in her life. Now that Paola Ford had arrived in her life, Emily was more relaxed and had become quite attached to her teacher, as was evident from the fact that she talked about her extensively during their sessions.

But it had come to the point where Emily had started asking questions herself, approaching these visits with frustration and doubts and the need to understand. So, the doctor tried to find the simplest and sweetest words to explain to the little girl what, in her opinion, she was going through.

"Emily, you are not strange in any way. No different from any other child. The reason for our meetings is that you've been through a tough time because of what happened with your father. And I'm here to help you suffer less, to help you move forward. You're not the only child in the world growing up without a father. For example, my father worked in the military, and often I didn't hear from or see him for months. I also suffered a lot from this when I was little."

Emily's eyes widened. Dr. Jackson was sure the girl had heard that there were other children growing up without their fathers, and seeing the child's face light up upon hearing her story only reinforced how important it was for Emily to know that divorce, abandonment, and loss were common occurrences and that she wasn't the only child forced to go through this painful experience.

Dr. Jackson strongly believed that Emily's trauma could be overcome with love. Emily needed to fill the void of love that had been taken from her.

"You are not to blame for what happened," Dr. Jackson said, fierce but gentle. "And even though your father is gone, don't doubt that he loves you, that your mother loves you, and that everyone who comes into your life cares about you. Now there's also Ms. Ford. But I understand that you would like to go back to your normal life, just like any other child. Going to school like everyone else and playing with other children. It will happen soon. Very soon. I am here to make that possible as soon as possible."

The disappearances in the house had drastically decreased as well, according to Valerie. This meant there had been improvements. There was still the mystery of where young Emily had stashed or discarded those things, what had triggered that behavior in the child's mind, and, most importantly, how to help her control that impulse, an impulse that, at Emily's tender age, she was unaware of having. It hadn't been explained to her with sincerity. And this was the most difficult thing Dr. Jackson felt she had to address in her therapy: explaining to Emily her problem and teaching her how to control it. And she had some ideas about how to go about doing so.

Chapter 6

New London, Connecticut
October 31, 2001

On Halloween, Valerie and Emily went to New London. Dr Jackson had proposed to Valerie that she take Emily trick-or-treating in the neighborhood near her office so that she could observe Emily's behavior from afar in a festive setting. This particular neighborhood had a reputation for going all out on Halloween. Plus, it was a safe area for kids to roam around freely, knocking on strangers' doors and demanding candy.

Valerie had sewn a stunning fairy princess costume for Emily—a pink satin dress edged with rhinestones, a magic wand tipped with a pink star, and delicate translucent wings wired to the back of the dress.

Emily could barely contain her excitement over the costume and all the candy she'd get in New London. The previous year, she and her mother had gone from door to door in their small neighborhood in Mystic, and she still remarked on how much candy she had collected during that house-to-house hunt. In New London, Emily announced that she'd collect at least twice as much.

Valerie parked the truck in the parking lot of the building in which Dr. Jackson's office was located. Emily hopped eagerly out of the car, ready to walk the two blocks to the "Halloween Town," as she called it.

The afternoon passed quickly. Emily went from house to house, while, behind her, a short distance away, Valerie and Dr. Jackson observed her interactions with the homeowners and the other trick-or-treaters.

"At home with Emily, Mrs. Barton, how is it going?" Dr. Jackson asked.

Valerie smiled tentatively. "Better, although it still happens that one of her hairbands or other small things disappear. It's not easy living in this situation, but I see significant progress. And I'm sure it's thanks to you."

Dr. Jackson took a deep breath then, indicating that she was about to say something that was difficult to explain. "I think at this point, we need to find a way to explain the situation to Emily so that we can then introduce a method to control her behavior."

Valerie felt a throb of anxiety. She'd left her cigarettes at home and was feeling the effects of nicotine withdrawal. "What do you mean by a method to control?"

"I have some ideas about it." Dr. Jackson's tone was diplomatic. "They are exercises. I believe that, at the root of all this, in the child's subconscious, there is a desire to make things disappear or maybe a belief that she is secretly guarding things. I've noticed that most of the items Emily makes disappear are objects she cares about, objects she is attracted to. So, I think we need to find a way to help her feel more secure when she is in front of or in possession of one of these items."

"I don't understand," Valerie said, confused.

"I mean . . ." Dr. Jackson paused, as if trying to find the right words to explain herself better. "Okay, let's give an example. We know how much Emily loves that little magic wand she's holding in her hand right now." She pointed to Emily, who stood not far away. "And since she loves it so much, it probably means that, tonight, that magic wand will disappear. And I firmly believe the reason behind it is her fear of losing what she loves but, at the same time, her feeling like she deserves to be abandoned. And it's that part of her, hidden somewhere inside her, that's been making objects disappear lately, as if, in the end, everyone and everything should abandon her."

Valerie crossed her arms protectively over her chest. "What do you think is the right thing to do?"

"Just anticipate it, for now," the doctor replied. "I still need to come up with a way she will relate to in order explain what's happening without her realizing it. And then we'll teach her a way to control that impulse, to understand when there's a risk it might happen and give her a tool to control it."

"What kind of tool are you thinking of?" Valerie asked.

There were a few seconds of silence. Valerie fixed her eyes on Emily, who was studying a jack-o-lantern on the doorstep of the latest house in her search.

"I'm working on it," Dr. Jackson finally answered. "I'm reading a lot about it. Many studies by other colleagues have dealt with similar cases."

Valerie nodded and then smiled; Emily's candy bag was getting heavier and harder for her to carry. "It's getting late," she said, checking the time.

Dr. Jackson nodded and Valerie beckoned Emily to start walking back to the office.

* * *

As soon as they were back at their house, Valerie went for her pack of Marlboro, as Emily spilled her candies noisily onto the kitchen table. Valerie lit a cigarette and took a long drag before going to retrieve a large glass bowl from the pantry.

Placing the bowl in the center of the table, she said, "Put all the candy in this container. Then, let's make a pact about how much and when you can have the treats. I wouldn't want you to end up with a stomachache."

"Sure, sure!" Emily replied, scooping handfuls of sweets into the large bowl.

"And then dinner and bed," Valerie went on. "Tomorrow is a school day. Your teacher will be here early, as usual."

"Of course, Mom," Emily said as she dropped the last little package of Twizzlers into the bowl. Those were her favorite.

* * *

The following morning, Valerie had started preparing breakfast when she made a mental note that the bowl on the table was empty. "Emily!" she called out.

No response.

"Emily!" Valerie called again.

The sound of her daughter's feet hitting the floor upstairs confirmed she had heard her. She listened as Emily hurried down the stairs. Emily rushed into the kitchen, hair disheveled, and her eyes locked immediately on the empty bowl.

"Did you take them?" Valerie asked firmly. "Don't tell me you ate them all!"

Emily, still visibly groggy, stared at her mother and then back at the empty bowl in silent confusion.

"Emily, answer me," Valerie said again, this time with a gentler tone.

Emily seemed to realize what had happened, and she bit her lip, tears welling in her eyes. Her gaze remained fixed, almost hypnotized, on the bowl that had been filled with Halloween candies the previous evening.

Valerie didn't wait for her response and left the room.

* * *

Emily remained in the kitchen, in silence, trying to remember what had happened. She had gone to bed the previous evening, leaving the bowl full on the table. She had eaten only one little Hershey bar, just as her mother had allowed her to, nothing else. She remembered falling asleep in her bed shortly after. Now she stood there, in front of the empty bowl.

A tear rolled down her small, sad face.

A little later, when Paola Ford arrived for her lessons, Emily was still sitting at the table, ready for her lesson but still distraught. The teacher seemed to notice something was wrong and asked if everything was okay.

Emily looked at her with teary eyes. "It happened again," she replied.

"What happened again?" Paola asked, puzzled.

"All the Halloween candies disappeared," she said with frustration. Emily knew her teacher knew about all the missing things because she often spoke with Dr. Jackson.

Ms. Ford made a sad face, reached across the table, and took Emily's hand. "Sweetie, don't worry," she reassured her. "The time will come when this won't happen anymore. We're all working toward that. Dr. Jackson and I, along with your mother, are doing everything we can to help you with this . . . to help you recover from this thing," Paola said.

Emily burst into tears and flung her arms around her teacher's neck. Just then, her mother came storming into the room, red in the face. "Ms. Ford, may I speak with you for a moment?"

* * *

Valerie stalked to the kitchen with the young teacher on her heels and terror gripping her heart. She'd overheard everything from her workroom. Ms. Ford had said "recover," which practically told Emily that she was sick. That wasn't her role. *She is just supposed to be a teacher,* Valerie thought, her face burning.

Valerie looked the teacher straight in the eyes and kept her voice low so as not to be overhead by Emily. "Ms. Ford, I don't believe it's your role to talk to Emily about her problem."

"Yes, but Emily–"

"But nothing, Ms. Ford," Valerie hissed. "Your role is to teach my child history, science, grammar, and math. The psychologist is Dr. Jackson, not you."

Paola nodded and lowered her gaze, visibly cowed. "I . . . I am so sorry. It won't happen again," she said.

"That's right, Ms. Ford, because if it *does* happen again, I am going to request a new teacher for Emily. Do you understand me?"

Paola looked up at her. "Yes, of course, I apologize again."

Valerie wasn't sure she was satisfied with that answer, but she decided to accept the apology for now and just keep a more watchful eye on Ms. Ford's interactions with her daughter. Emily would need some undivided attention from her later. She'd have to save today's soaps until tomorrow night. Tonight, she and Emily would do something special, play a card game perhaps, to take Emily's mind off the missing candy.

"Fine," she said. "That's fine, Ms. Ford. Please go back to Emily and do your job."

The teacher wiped the tears from her eyes and straightened her shoulders. She spun on her heels and left the kitchen. Valerie went for her cigarettes. She didn't usually smoke while she was working to avoid getting smoke smell on the fabric, but she'd wash her hands well. She just really needed a cigarette right now.

* * *

Autumn passed and the Christmas season arrived without any further disappearances, but truth be told, there wasn't much left of Emily's belongings that could go missing. Her candy had been the last to vanish. On Christmas morning, Emily woke up at the crack of dawn and rushed downstairs.

Weeks before, with the help of Ms. Ford, she had written a letter to Santa Claus. She had asked for many things, everything she needed for her chemistry experiments, her great passion. But above all, she really wished for her father's return. She had written that only that would be enough, and it didn't matter if she received nothing else; that would be the most beautiful gift. The letter had brought tears to her teacher's eyes.

When Emily entered the living room where Valerie had decorated a modest Christmas tree, she immediately noticed a long, wrapped tube underneath it. Nothing else. Her heart sank. A microscope would not fit in that tube. Nothing she had asked for would fit in such a small tube. She looked at it with confusion and picked it up. The tag read, "For Emily from Santa Claus."

She unwrapped it and found a cardboard tube. She inspected it cautiously and saw a cap at one end. She opened it and pulled out the contents. It was a poster. A giant periodic table. She was studying it, fascinated, when Valerie appeared in the room, smiling.

"Do you like it?" her mother asked.

Emily nodded without taking her eyes off the gift. Then she looked at her mother. "Why didn't Santa get me anything on my list?"

"Maybe Santa was worried about getting you too many things right now, you know, because of what might happen to them," Valerie carefully responded. "But that periodic table, now that's something, isn't it?"

"Can we hang it in my room?" the little girl asked.

"Of course, honey. Of course, we can. In fact, let's do it right now." Valerie rose to locate some tape.

Mother and daughter hurried upstairs and chose the most suitable wall to hang the periodic table. They settled on the one in front of Emily's bed, above her dresser. Valerie had secured the top left corner to the wall when Emily, who held out the tape reel, asked with concern, "Do you think I'll make this poster disappear like everything else?"

Her mother didn't answer immediately. Once the poster was secured on the wall, she turned to her daughter. "Let's do something," she said, motioning for the little girl to sit on the bed. "I've got an idea."

"What is it?" Emily asked.

Valerie paused again. "You know what experiments are, right?" she asked. "Like the chemistry ones you enjoy so much?"

"Yes, of course."

"Well, we can do a little experiment and try to make things stop disappearing," Valerie continued.

Emily perked up at this. "What kind of experiment?"

Her mother smiled and stroked her head. "Has Dr. Jackson told you how special you are?" she asked sweetly.

"Yes. She told me I'm afraid of losing things I like, and because of that, I make them disappear without realizing it. Maybe I have some magic power?"

"Yes," Valerie confirmed, nodding vigorously. "You have a kind of magic power. But it's a power that makes you suffer, so we need to control it."

"How?" Emily asked hopefully.

"Let's try a little exercise and see how it goes. When you see something you really like, something you care about a lot, stop for a moment. Take a deep breath and count. Count to ten. Focus on a point and count. Any point that can distract you."

"Why?" Emily asked, confused.

Valerie paused. "Because it's a way to control your emotions. This is what Dr. Jackson said might help," she answered.

Emily nodded, even though she didn't fully understand the meaning of her mother's words.

"You have to stay calm," her mother soothed. "I'm here to protect you. Nothing and no one will ever harm you. And I will never leave you. Never. And all of this will pass soon. You must trust me. Okay? You know you can trust me more than anyone else, right?"

Emily nodded again. "Can we try the experiment now? I don't want Santa's gift to disappear."

Valerie smiled. "Yes, let's try it right away."

Emily stood up, scanning the room. She needed to find a point to focus on to start counting. Up to ten or more. She pointed at a tile on the floor in the corner of the room. It was different from the others, chipped. She focused on the cracked grain and began to count.

"One, two, three, four, five, six, seven, eight, nine, ten." Emily spoke in a whisper, her eyes half-closed, as if making a wish. Then she continued, still looking at the same tile. She kept counting over and over.

Her mother stood there behind her, in silence. When Emily felt it was safe to stop counting, she looked up at the periodic table poster and sighed with relief to see it still hung there.

Her mother wrapped an arm around her from behind and stroked her hair off her forehead. "I won't let anyone hurt you or take you away from me, my little flower. Stay calm, I'll never leave you. It'll just be me and you, forever."

* * *

Even though school was still out until after the New Year, on December 27, Paola Ford rang the doorbell at nine o'clock, asking to see Emily. She said she was passing by and wanted to give Emily a little gift. Valerie permitted her inside without much courtesy. They generally exchanged few words following "the incident." Valerie had never been very fond of the young woman, finding her intrusive and unprofessional, especially when, in Valerie's opinion, she crossed the boundaries of her role as a teacher—just like she was doing now.

She trailed after Ms. Ford as the teacher approached Emily, who sat in the living room looking at the TV on which a gameshow was playing. Valerie stalked to her workroom, from which she could hear every word exchanged in the living room.

"Good morning, Emily!" the young woman said to the little girl. "How as your Christmas!"

"I got a cool poster from Santa, and I ate lots of yummy treats," Emily shared.

Valerie smiled, feeling triumphant.

"You know," Paola said, "I brought you a little gift, too. It's nothing big–not a microscope," she said with an uneasy laugh.

Valerie straightened, listening intently.

"A gift?" Emily asked eagerly.

"Yes," the teacher replied.

There was a momentary rustling of wrapping paper before Emily exclaimed, "A pen and a journal!"

"Yes, and the pen even has my name and phone number engraved on it. The office where I work usually gives me plenty, and I thought I'd include one for you along with the journal."

Valerie's hackles rose. She heard Emily's feet hit the floor and knew she'd jumped up to hug her teacher.

"Thank you! This makes me so happy!" the girl said.

Valerie scowled in disappointment and thumped her fist on the worktable.

When she heard Ms. Ford leaving, Valerie didn't go to the door to say goodbye. She knew she wouldn't be able to hide her animosity. The teacher had basically given her daughter her phone number, which clearly meant Ms. Ford wanted Emily to call her. *How unprofessional!* she huffed silently, feeling a protective urge. She thought to go smoke a cigarette, but instead she brought a glass of milk and a few sugar cookies to Emily.

“Ms. Ford gave me this cool journal and a pen!” Emily exclaimed, showing the gifts to her mother.

Valerie smiled at her daughter. “How lovely. Can I see the pen?”

Emily handed it to her. The barrel read, “Paola Ford. Connecticut Department of Education.” Her direct phone number was stamped below.

Valerie handed the pen back to her daughter and returned to her worktable. She sat there, pondering what to do for a few minutes, then glanced at the clock and suddenly stood up.

She went to the phone and dialed Ms. Ford’s number.

* * *

The rest of the week was interminably long for Emily, but then she and her mother spent a peaceful New Year’s Eve together. They took a stroll downtown and bought some sweets to enjoy that evening while waiting for the New Year to arrive. Valerie had promised that Emily could stay up until midnight that evening to see the ball drop, but Emily dozed off on the couch forty minutes before midnight while her mother sat absently stroking her back with one hand and clutching a glass of whiskey in the other.

When Emily woke the next day, she first checked to make sure she still had her pen and then looked up to make sure her poster was still there. The journal had already gone missing a few days earlier. Satisfied she hadn’t yet made the pen or poster disappear, she went down for breakfast. She looked at the new 2002 calendar on the refrigerator. Her vacation had been mostly boring, and she couldn’t wait to get back to her lessons.

The next morning, January 2, Emily dressed quickly and sat at the dining table, anticipating her teacher's arrival. Yes, she'd missed learning over the vacation, but truth be told, she missed Ms. Ford even more.

"Are you ready to get back to your lessons?" her mother asked she poured herself another cup of coffee.

"I am!" replied Emily, scribbling in her school notebook with her pen, which she hadn't let go of since she'd received the gift a week before. She even slept with it for fear of losing it. She sat on her bed every night, holding the pen close to her chest, and staring at the chipped tile in the corner of her room as she counted to ten multiple times. When she woke up and still had the pen, she'd proudly tell her mother that the experiment was working. The pen hadn't disappeared.

Now Emily sat waiting for her teacher, happy and serene in a way she hadn't been in a while. The suffering caused by her father's absence in those months had paradoxically been alleviated by her inexplicable situation and her desire to overcome it.

At five past nine, her mother entered the living room, looking puzzled. "Weird. Ms. Ford hasn't arrived yet."

"Maybe she got caught in traffic," Emily suggested without looking up from her doodles.

"Maybe," her mother replied before returning to the kitchen.

At 9:20, Emily heard Valerie pick up the wall-mounted phone in the kitchen. Her mother dialed, but it seemed no one answered; Emily heard the phone being replaced in the cradle a moment later.

Valerie came scurrying out of the kitchen and headed to her workroom, returning with a sheet of paper a few seconds later. Emily rose and followed her to the kitchen doorway, tucking herself against the living room wall to listen in. This close to the phone, she could faintly make out the female voice that answered her mother's phone call after a couple of rings. "Department of Education, how can I help you?"

Her mother explained that Paola Ford hadn't shown up for her lessons with Emily. The woman on the other end promised to look into it and said she would contact Valerie when they had more information.

Hours passed, but no one called back. Emily felt restless, and Valerie explained to her that, most likely, Ms. Ford wouldn't be coming to give her the usual lesson that day. Emily held on to the pen more tightly.

It was only in the afternoon that the phone finally rang. The caller was the same woman from the Department of Education. Ms. Ford still hadn't contacted them, and they had tried to reach her on her cell phone without success. As soon as they could, they would discuss the matter with her to find out what had prompted her to miss the lesson without notice.

Emily tried to console herself by reading the pen's inscription over and over again.

* * *

The following day, exactly at nine o'clock, the doorbell rang. Valerie answered and found herself face to face with a slender, middle-aged woman with short black hair and very thick glasses.

"Hello, Valerie Barton?" the woman inquired.

"Yes, who are you?" Valerie asked.

"My name is Mandy Monroe," replied the woman. "I'm the substitute teacher."

"A substitute?" Valerie asked with a puzzled look.

"Yes, from what I understand, Ms. Ford is unavailable."

Valerie invited the teacher into the living room and went to call Emily from upstairs. When the girl stood before the new teacher, she looked surprised. "Where's Ms. Ford?" she asked, visibly confused.

"You must be Emily," said Ms. Monroe with a smile. "Nice to meet you. I'm Ms. Monroe. I'll be here as a substitute for Ms. Ford for a few days."

"Is she sick?" Emily asked.

Mrs. Monroe nodded. "Yes. I think she's not feeling very well. Can you show me where you usually have our lessons?"

Emily led her to the living room table. She placed her notebook in front of one of the chairs and gestured to the one next to it, indicating where Ms. Ford usually sat.

After asking Emily about what she had learned in the past few months and what she was currently studying, Ms. Monroe picked up where her colleague had left off.

Valerie returned to her workroom, satisfied with this turn of events.

* * *

Days passed, and each day, Emily hoped for Ms. Ford's return, but it was always and only Ms. Monroe who arrived at the door.

A week later, Emily woke up, and before her usual lesson, she checked for her pen. It wasn't in her hand or somewhere under the blankets as it usually was. She threw the covers off and looked everywhere, including under the bed. Then she checked for it among her school papers and notes.

Nothing. She scrambled back to her room, dumping out her nightstand and dresser drawers in increasing panic.

"Mom, Mom!" she called out in desperation.

By the time Valerie entered her daughter's room, out of breath from rushing, Emily was staring at her tile, counting, hands clenched against her chest, swaying back and forth. She had reached thirty-six when Valerie came up behind her and placed a hand on her shoulder.

The child turned, her eyes filled with tears, and looked at her mother. "It happened again," she said, her voice broken by sobs. "It happened again."

Valerie's miserable expression told Emily she understood. Her mother embraced her tightly. "Don't worry, my little flower," she whispered gently. "Don't worry. I'm still here."

Chapter 7

MYSTIC, CONNECTICUT
AUGUST 11, 2011

Exactly eleven years had passed since the day Emily had awakened to discover that her father had abandoned her, never to return. After the loss of her teacher's pen, there had been no more disappearances. Anyway, there wasn't much for her to lose. Emily had basically stopped acquiring things, intentionally keeping her possessions to a bare minimum. If she saw something she liked in a store, she'd walk right by it. If someone offered her a gift, she would politely decline.

On those rare occasions when she did come into possession of an item with particular sentimental value, generally a small gift from her mother, she would sit down, usually in her room, fixate on something, like her tile, and count. The counting had also become her go-to habit any time she felt out of sorts. As far as she could tell, the coping mechanism had been a success, and Emily had been able to keep those few personal items without any of them seemingly disappearing into thin air.

Ms. Ford had never returned, and after completing elementary school at home, Emily had returned to a regular classroom through middle school and high school. She liked having friends again, but she never invited them to her house and seldom went to theirs.

Valerie continued her work as a seamstress, managing to support herself and her daughter without her husband's financial assistance. Fortunately, their small house had already been paid off with money Albert had inherited from his parents prior to his abandoning of his family, and the taxes on the property were minimal. Albert's leftover inheritance was enough to cover them for a long while. Emily recalled that, back when she was in fifth grade, she'd overhead Ms. Monroe ask Valerie why she didn't try to track her husband down, at least for child support, and Valerie had simply replied that she was content with the way things were.

When Emily was a little older, Valerie had confided in her that she preferred handling everything herself, rather than dealing with the man. "Men aren't all they are cracked up to be," she'd told her one day while they were eating ice cream at the Drawbridge. "You and I are independent women. You, my little flower, don't need a man to be a success. And I'll always support you in whatever way I can. You really don't need more than that."

Emily had responded, "But, Mom, I *do* imagine myself getting married someday–and having kids. Wouldn't you want that for me?"

Valerie had bristled a bit at that and then flashed a smile. "Oh, yes, sure, of course. But you *must* hold out for true love and not give anyone else the time of day. When you find that someone special, it will be like you've been hit by a bolt of lightning. But be careful, because that bolt may also suggest potential disaster."

Emily had laughed at that, but she took her mother's words to heart.

Now, with those eleven years behind her, Emily was preparing for her senior year of high school, which would begin in three weeks. Her passion for chemistry hadn't diminished, and she had long ago decided that she wanted to major in pharmacy to become a researcher and discover new pharmaceutical treatments. It had been her dream for as long as she could remember. Emily had clear plans for her future, but she also knew that she didn't want to stray too far from her mother. It had always been just the two of them, and Valerie had dedicated her life to raising her. She had never remarried or even dated other men.

Emily, now an attractive young woman, had turned the heads of many high-school classmates, but she had never been interested in any of the boys. Although many of her schoolmates had asked her out for ice cream or a stroll along the river, Emily was almost entirely occupied with and focused on her studies. They brought her comfort.

Only twelve more months stood between her and her dreams. She planned to apply to a few universities in Connecticut by the December deadline, but there was really only one university she wanted to attend—Yale. Her grades had consistently been among the highest in her high school class, so she was sure she'd get accepted. However, she would need to be awarded a needs-based scholarship to actually be able to afford it.

Yale University wasn't just one of the most prestigious in the world; it was also only a few miles away from Mystic. This would allow her to stay close to her mother and minimize expenses during her years of university studies.

On that Saturday, August 11, Emily and her mother went downtown for their final back-to-school shopping. They bought notebooks, pens, pencils, and a new shoulder bag for her books. After shopping, they got ice cream at Drawbridge Ice Cream and stopped to enjoy it in front of the drawbridge spectacle. It was a tradition they had maintained since Emily was a little girl, and even though it didn't have the same effect on Emily as it used to, her mother wanted to keep the tradition alive.

"I'm not a little kid anymore, Mom. Can we eat our ice cream while walking along Main Street?" Emily suggested.

Valerie chuckled. "I know you're not a little kid anymore. But you know, you'll always be my little girl," Valerie replied, hugging her daughter.

Mother and daughter sat beside each other, gazing at the river.

"You know," Emily said after a while, "I've noticed you haven't talked to Aunt Anna on the phone in months."

"I called her the other day while you were grocery shopping," Valerie responded.

"How's she doing?"

Valerie shrugged. "Same as usual. A few aches and pains, but she doesn't complain. Your aunt never complains about anything. She's a strong and proud woman."

Emily licked a drop of melted ice cream off the side of her cone. "I was thinking that, after graduation, I'd like to visit her. What do you think? We could go together. After I get my driver's license, I could drive. It's not that far to Florida, about fifteen hours. Would you like that?"

Valerie remained silent for a moment before responding, "I don't know. My sister isn't an easy person. I'm not sure how much she'd appreciate having us visit. We couldn't afford to go to her all these years, but she's never really invited us, to be honest."

"Why do you think she's never invited us?" Emily asked, curious.

"I don't know," Valerie replied with a tinge of sadness. "Maybe not to offend us knowing our financial difficulties, or because she's not swimming in wealth herself and doesn't want to show us her living conditions."

Emily nodded and didn't press the issue further.

* * *

On September 5, Emily showed up on the first day of her final year of high school dressed in pink. It had become a tradition for her. Since that morning eleven years earlier when she had hoped her father would show up to wish her a happy start to the school year, she had never stopped dressing in pink on the first day of school and on other important occasions. And just like all those eleven years before, her father didn't show up.

Emily joined her small group of friends, Clare, Mary, and Jessica, by their lockers. She'd known them in first grade, and they quickly rekindled their friendship when she went back to regular classes. The first two were dating guys from the school from the previous year, while Jessica had recently ended a relationship that had started in middle school.

It often happened that the other three acted as intermediaries for guys who wanted to get to know Emily. Unlike her friends, Emily had never had any romantic experiences. She had never kissed a boy or even walked hand in hand. She'd never met a boy she'd been attracted to more than she was attracted to maintaining the status quo.

Her friends had scolded her for being too picky and told her there was nothing wrong with gaining some experience or giving someone interesting a chance. They had also scolded her because some of the cutest guys in school had tried to approach her, and they wouldn't have hesitated to date them.

But Emily was waiting for true love, like her mother had described to her. When the right guy came along, she would know. There was no rush, and she believed that later was better.

Romance, boys, and "youthful discoveries" would distract her from her academic goals. She needed to hit a home run with her college essays. She had to impress Yale and make them want her, at any cost.

"Sandy Barton and her pink dress arriving on the red carpet!" Clare exclaimed when she saw Emily.

The four friends burst into laughter before hugging tightly. Emily's friends had given her the nickname Sandy, like the character from the musical *Grease*, because of her difficulty in letting herself go with guys.

"So, it's our graduation year," Jessica said, pretending to cry and hugging her friends tightly. "The last one, dear friends. And then we'll have to part ways forever."

"We know what Emily wants to do in life. But what about you?" Mary asked the girls. "What do you plan to study after graduation?"

"I want to become a doctor!" Jessica replied seriously.

"I plan to marry a billionaire!" Clare said, making them all erupt in giggles.

"Meanwhile, I have exciting news!" Mary chimed in, pulling out a brand-new driver's license from her backpack.

Jessica snatched it from her hands and stared at it with excitement. "This is great! Now you can take all of us for a spin! We can go to Mason's Island every Friday for ice cream and sunbathing! I should get my license after Christmas break."

"And what about you, Sandy?" Jessica asked, turning her gaze toward Emily. "When do you plan to get your driver's license?"

"I don't think I'll be able to for a while," Emily replied. She had discussed it with her mother, who had explained that they were going through another period of financial difficulty so driving lessons were out of the question; they would need to wait until after graduation.

"I got an iPhone for my birthday!" Clare announced, showing off a brand-new iPhone 4S with a pink case. "It has a virtual assistant called Siri."

And there it is, Emily thought, *something else I don't have.* She thought she might be the only kid her age without a phone but told herself it didn't matter. She had her goals, and she liked to think that one day, once her dreams were realized, she would have everything she wanted—and she would be able to hold on to it all.

At that moment, the school bell rang, and all the students who had been congregating at their lockers started making their way toward their classes.

Emily had chemistry as her first class, and as always, she sat in one of the front-row desks. Sitting next to her was a young man she had never seen before. He smiled at her, and Emily returned the gesture.

"Robert," the young man said, extending his hand.

Emily stared at the outstretched hand, shook it, and then looked up, noticing his big green eyes, one of which was partially hidden behind a long blond lock of hair. Her heart skipped a beat.

"I'm new," the boy continued, just as their chemistry teacher, Mr. Maxwell, entered the classroom. "Just moved here from England."

"Pleasure," Emily whispered, releasing her hand and shifting her gaze to the teacher.

After the morning classes, at lunchtime, Emily and her friends sat at a secluded table in the school cafeteria, as they had always done.

"Now, tell me, girls," Jessica began as soon as she sat down at the table, "who among you hasn't noticed the super sexy new arrival from across the ocean?"

"Robert?" Emily asked impulsively.

"You already know his name?" Jessica asked, looking surprised and grabbing her friend's wrist.

"Yes," Emily confirmed. "He was sitting next to me in chemistry class. He introduced himself."

"Oh my God!" Jessica exclaimed, looking upward. "I knew I should have taken chemistry this year. I felt it!"

The other three girls to burst into laughter.

Robert became the topic of their entire lunch conversation. Emily's three friends couldn't stop talking about him–his looks, his accent, his manners. The young man had been at the school for only four hours and had already become the object of desire for most of the girls in the school.

Meanwhile, Emily found herself most intrigued by their shared passion and the proficiency in chemistry Robert had displayed in class that morning. Or at least, that's what she tried to convince herself of.

* * *

A month passed, and Emily always looked forward to her chemistry class, not only because of her passion for the subject but also because chemistry class meant seeing Robert.

It was a Monday, and Robert arrived with a small rectangular box, wrapped and tied with ribbon. He sat down beside her and handed her the gift.

"I heard that a couple of weeks ago was your birthday," he said, looking embarrassed. "Here's a late present."

Emily stared at him, surprised and speechless. Her first impulse was to decline the gift, but then she glanced at the small package. She picked it up without responding and unwrapped it with shaking hands. From the box, she pulled out a rectangular ruler printed with a replica of the periodic table.

Tears welled up in Emily's eyes. She jumped to her feet, rushed out of the classroom, and locked herself in the bathroom. She stared at herself in the mirror, trying to stem her tears. She was embarrassed by her reaction. She looked at the gift in her hands again, still moist with her tears, and smiled. She clutched it tightly between her hands and shifted her gaze to one of the floor tiles. Then, she began to count. She counted up to one hundred.

The happiness that the thoughtful gesture gave her mixed with the fear that Robert's sweet gift might trigger a relapse; it had been over a decade since she'd made anything special to her "disappear," but this gift felt *extra* special.

At that moment, as she whispered the count while staring at the floor, Emily realized that she felt a strong emotional pull toward Robert, one she didn't have a name for yet. It was the first time she had felt such an emotion, and it scared her.

Emily decided not to share this feeling with anyone. She didn't want to hear her friends' gossip or her mother's concern. She returned quietly to class and sat down next to Robert. She couldn't look at him, and she didn't feel his eyes on her. She wondered if he felt as embarrassed as she did.

Only when Mr. Maxwell turned to write a formula on the chalkboard did Emily slowly lean toward Robert.

"Thank you for the gift," she whispered. "And . . . I'm sorry for my reaction. I didn't expect it. That's it."

Robert smiled without taking his eyes off the chalkboard. "I hope you like it," he whispered back.

Emily smiled and lowered her gaze to the ruler on her desk. "Very much," she said, suppressing a grin as her face burned with embarrassment.

Emily decided to keep the gift a secret as well. She knew that if she shared it with her friends, they would tease her relentlessly. She also chose not to tell her mother; she didn't want her mother to worry about any potential psychological effects the gift might cause her. Emily felt confident she could control her impulses with her counting technique.

At the end of the lesson, Robert stood up and left the classroom. Emily did the same and found him standing outside the door, waiting for her.

"Hi, Emily," he said, his voice silky and suggestive.

"Hi, Robert," Emily replied shyly, clutching her books to her chest.

He took a step forward. "I wanted to ask if you'd like to study together for next week's chemistry test."

Emily contemplated. Of course, she wanted to. But she also thought about all the complications it might bring. "I don't think it's a good idea," she concluded, stepping back. "I'm not used to studying in groups for tests. But thanks for the offer."

The boy looked surprised and bewildered. Emily turned away, leaving Robert alone in the middle of the school corridor.

* * *

In the weeks that followed, Emily and Robert spoke very little. Emily would enter the classroom, take her seat, try to focus on the lesson, and leave as soon as the bell rang. Whenever she saw Robert in the hall or schoolyard, her heart would race . She would turn red and find it difficult to speak. Then, for the first time since starting high school, she received an A minus on a chemistry test, and it nearly devastated her. She felt that Robert and her feelings for him were jeopardizing her academic career and, more importantly, her chance at the scholarship to Yale, her ultimate goal.

Valerie also seemed to notice Emily's long silences and constant distraction. She asked Emily if something was wrong, and Emily, sensing that Valerie was a little too close to the truth—that a boy was the reason—Emily always replied that it was just stress from the heavy workload of her final year of high school. However, Emily knew that mother didn't buy the excuse.

As Christmastime approached, Emily had had enough of trying to ignore her feelings for Robert and decided to reciprocate his gesture. With the money she'd saved from little cash gifts she'd received over the years from her mother, she purchased a tumbled piece of rose quartz encased in a small glass box from one of the shops on Main Street, while her mom was busy buying fabric in another store. Rose quartz was known as the "love stone," and she believed that Robert, with his shared passion for chemistry and gemstones, would understand its significance.

It was a genuine declaration of love from Emily. She believed the feeling was mutual, but Robert had stopped trying to talk to her about anything of consequence. Emily worried that he thought she wasn't interested in him. This gift would tell him otherwise. When she got home, she hid the small box in the back of her bedroom drawer, waiting for the day before Christmas break to give it him.

The evening before the break was to begin, Emily went to her room after dinner. She took the glass box out of her drawer, as she had done every evening since purchasing it, and placed it on her nightstand. She lay down, put her hands on her chest, and stared at a small imperfection in the ceiling's paint, and began counting, "One, two, three, four . . ." She counted without stopping. Emily felt terrified that this precious gift, which meant so much to her, might disappear along with most everything she ever cared about. She counted relentlessly until she fell asleep.

The next morning, she woke up early, eyes half-closed, and looked at her nightstand. The glass box was gone. She sat up abruptly, confused and terrified. She looked under the nightstand, behind it, and in the drawers. There was no sign of the box. She crawled around her room, searching frantically among her meager belongings.

"No, no, no . . ." she repeated incessantly as she desperately looked for any trace of it. Finding nothing in her room, she rushed downstairs, calling, "Mom! Mom!"

In the kitchen, Emily found her mother sitting at the table. In front of her, in the center of the table, was the box with the pink gem inside.

"Sit down, Emily," Valerie said calmly.

The young woman sat at the opposite end of the table, her gaze fixed on the glass box.

"Who is this gift for, young lady?" her mother asked.

There were a few seconds of silence.

"It's for Robert," Emily replied without lifting her gaze.

"And who is Robert?" her mother pressed. "And why are you giving a gift to one of your schoolmates?"

More silence followed, and then, for the first time since entering the room, Emily looked up at her mother. “Because he gave me a gift months ago, and I wanted to reciprocate.”

“Are you in love?” Valerie asked, her voice trembling.

“I think so,” Emily answered, lowering her gaze once more.

Valerie bit out, “You *think*?”

“I know I like him a lot,” she said, swallowing a lump in her throat. “And I believe he likes me a lot too. I’m pretty sure it’s love.”

Valerie let out a long sigh. “Why didn’t you ever tell me about this?”

Emily told the truth: “Because I was afraid of your reaction. I was afraid you’d think that he’d take me away from maintaining my GPA and working on my college applications.”

Shifting in her chair and looking intently at Emily, Valerie said, “I’m very disappointed that you kept this from me. I thought that after everything we’ve been through together, all that I’ve done over the years to raise you to be healthy and honest, especially with me, we had established a relationship of mutual trust.”

Emily looked up at her mother again, tears welling up in her eyes. “Mom, I trust you,” she said almost desperately. “I love you. I was just afraid you wouldn’t approve. For the academics, the scholarship, and everything else. I was afraid you’d be angry because this could have distracted me.”

Valerie took another deep breath. Then she pushed the small box toward Emily, got up, and left the room.

Emily covered her face with her hands and began to cry.

* * *

When Emily arrived at school later that morning, she scanned the crowd of students for Robert. There was no sign of him in front of the school, so she entered and went to search near the lockers.

Turning the corner of the hallway, she spotted him entering the combination at his locker. Emily took a deep breath, pulled the transparent box from her pocket, and approached him.

As Robert turned, he saw Emily approaching, and his face lit up. "Hey, Einstein." He had given her the nickname a few months earlier, but he hadn't used it much lately.

"Hi, Robert," she replied, holding out the gift.

The young man first looked at the small package, then at Emily's embarrassed face. "Is this for me?" he asked.

"Yes. I wanted to reciprocate your gift, so I thought that–"

Robert suddenly leaned in and kissed her.

Emily was taken aback, frozen by his unexpected but pleasant gesture. Then her face heated with excitement.

"Thank you, Emily," he whispered, kissing her again.

She lowered her head, momentarily rendered speechless. "I've never done this before," she said.

"What do you mean?" he asked, confused. "You've never kissed a guy before? Or what?"

She nodded.

Robert hugged her. "For a first timer, you're a pretty good kisser, Emily Barton," he whispered into her ear.

* * *

During the lunch hour, Emily and Robert were the talk of the cafeteria. When Emily arrived at her friends' table, she found them all excited.

"So, Sandy," Clare asked playfully, "what happened to all that talk about not wanting guys because you had to focus only on Yale and your scholarship?"

Emily felt herself blushing. "I don't know what you're talking about, Clare," she replied without looking up from her lunch tray.

"I'm talking about that study session this morning that *everyone* is talking about," her friend said, mimicking hugs and kisses while the others giggled.

Emily smiled. "It's complicated."

"Sandy Barton," Jessica exclaimed, raising her arms in disbelief, "for five years, you played hard to get, and then you ended up kissing the coolest guy in school in front of the lockers. I can't make sense of life!"

Emily didn't join in as her friends laughed. "I don't know what happened to me, girls. I'm feeling something I've never felt before. Unexpected. Not sought after. Robert is just . . ."

"Cool? Handsome? Sexy?" Mary asked teasingly.

"It's not that. He's just . . ." Emily replied, her sentence trailing off as she stared off into space.

"Oh my God," Clare exclaimed. "The girl is completely lost!"

It was true, Emily realized then. Before she knew it, she'd fallen deeply in love with Robert. Try as she might to ignore it, the young man occupied her every thought.

Then, a shiver ran down her spine. She knew this situation would distract her from her life's goals. Is this the disaster her mother had warned her? She was on the verge of achieving her dreams of getting a scholarship, and now she worried what would happen once that dream was realized. Would she and Robert be separated forever? Where would he go to continue his studies? Would they break up? Were they even together? Would he forget her? Would they never see each other again?

She felt foolish for these thoughts. It had only been a kiss. A tender moment. They had only talked for five minutes that morning.

"Earth to Sandy! Earth to Sandy!" Jessica exclaimed.

Emily smiled at her friends, her first smile since sitting down. "I'm here. It was just a kiss, girls. The year ends in six months. I'm submitting my application to Yale on Monday, and I know I'll be accepted. It's just a matter of getting enough need-based aid. I'm sure it'll come through. And who knows where Robert's going to be accepted. I'll have my career and life, and he'll have his. End of story," Emily concluded, trying to convince herself more than her friends.

Chapter 8

Emily and Robert soon became inseparable during school hours; they rarely met outside of school unless there was some school-themed event. Emily vowed to let nothing distract her from her goal. She had to finish her classes with the highest grades. She couldn't afford to stumble on any tests or school projects. That one A minus had been her last A minus.

Robert respected her determination. In the mornings, they met in front of the lockers, kissed, attended some classes together, and sometimes had lunch together. After school, they sat talking in the parking lot in his car before they kissed again and said their goodbyes.

When Valerie was out grocery shopping or running errands, Emily would call Robert from the kitchen phone to talk with him until she heard her mother's key jiggling at the front door. As in love as Emily knew they were, the two rarely discussed the future. Each time it came up, Emily changed the subject. She knew her fate in that story—or at least she thought she did.

If everything went according to plan, she would get accepted to Yale with enough needs-based aid for at least her first year. Robert, on the other hand, had only submitted applications to colleges in California, loving the idea of living on the West Coast. For Emily, their story would end with high school graduation, but she wanted to enjoy these fresh experiences until the end.

Sometimes, Robert would give her a flower or a small trinket, and Emily would secretly keep them in her room under her mattress. Every night before bed, she did her exercises. And it was working. Nothing Robert gave her vanished.

Emily was becoming a woman. Her fears were fading with time, and her confidence grew. She rarely thought about her father now, the father who had abandoned her without a backward glance.

Her relationship with Valerie had changed, too, but not for the worse. Now that her secret was out, Emily shared with her mother things that she and Robert talked about and little gestures he made toward her but kept the gifts he'd given her to herself. She didn't want to jinx it by saying out loud how much those silly little gifts meant to her.

Valerie would listen to her stories at dinner and relate them to some drama happening on the soaps, always reminding Emily that her career should come first. Emily always assured her that would be the case. Valerie seemed to believe her. She never questioned her daughter's determination to get into the most prestigious university on the East Coast, but she did caution Emily that feelings were difficult to predict and control. They *could* interfere with her plans.

Emily didn't see a future with Robert, so she wasn't concerned about her plans for the future getting waylaid. She also didn't see a traumatic ending their relationship; it was just young love, a romantic companionship in their senior year of high school. In mid-March, Emily had received acceptance letters to *all* the colleges she had applied to, but only one acceptance letter mattered: Yale's. She quickly set the wheels in motion for the financial assistance she'd need, and now it was just a waiting game. Whatever the outcome, the path she and Robert were on would soon split—and Robert would disappear from her life.

* * *

The morning of May 14, Robert did not arrive in front of the school on time. Emily looked for him at their usual place by the lockers, but he was not there. It had happened before; he was often late in the morning. Therefore, Emily did not worry.

First period that day was chemistry class, and Emily approached her usual seat.

On her desk was a white envelope with her name written on it. It was clearly Robert's handwriting; Emily knew it well. She took the envelope, glanced around to be sure no one was watching, and opened it.

Inside, on a sheet of white paper, were written a series of letter symbols for elements from the periodic table—Tungsten, Iodine, Yttrium, Oxygen, Uranium, Oxygen, Oxygen again, Thorium, Nitrogen, Cerium, Tungsten again, Iodine again, Thorium—interspersed with letters to spell out a message:

W I ll Y O U g O t O Th e d a N Ce W I Th me?

"Will you go to the dance with me?" Emily whispered aloud.

She felt a hand on her shoulder, and Robert sat down beside her. Emily didn't look up from the letter but placed a hand over her mouth, overcome with love. She had known this moment would come, that eventually she and Robert would go to prom together. But the way Robert had asked her had surprised and moved her. Her heart pounded in her chest. Staring at the letter, she began to count.

"Why are you counting?" Robert asked. "Did I make a mistake in the formula?"

Emily stopped. She had inadvertently practiced her mental exercise aloud. "Nothing. It's something silly," she replied, raising her gaze to meet his. "Yttrium and Einsteinium, Robert. Yttrium and Einsteinium!"

"Yes? Really?" Robert sounded surprised, as if wanting to make sure of her answer.

"Yes. I'd be honored to go to prom with you!" Emily replied, her voice filled with joy.

"Quiet, students!" Mr. Maxwell shouted.

Robert and Emily stopped talking, turned toward the teacher with smiles, and subtly touched knees under the desk.

Emily couldn't concentrate for even a minute during that class. Her thoughts scattered in every direction. What would she wear? How would her friends react to the news? What would her mother say?

She imagined the moment when Robert would come to pick her up, the classic photo together, their entrance into the party. Emily knew that more than half of the girls in school were envious of the fact that Robert had chosen to be with her, Emily Barton, who was not the least bit popular. Now she thought about what they would say when they saw her entering the prom next to the most desired guy in school. She absolutely had to have a beautiful dress.

* * *

On the way home, Emily considered how to share the news with her mother, but more importantly, how to ask her for a dress for the event. Valerie could sew her a princess-like dress if she wanted to. However, it would require a lot of fabric and various other materials, which Valerie would likely see as unnecessary and unexpected expenses. Emily was certain that a dress for her daughter's prom was not at the top of Valerie's list of priorities.

Once she crossed the threshold of her home, Emily rushed to the kitchen. Valerie was busy cooking dinner.

"How was your school day, honey?" her mother asked without turning from the kitchen counter.

"Same as usual," Emily said calmly. "But I have some exciting news."

Valerie stopped what she was doing and turned toward her daughter. "Tell me. What's the news?" she asked, a hint of tension in her voice.

Emily smiled at her mother, bringing her hands to her chest. "Robert asked me to go to the prom with him!" she exclaimed.

There were a few seconds of silence as Valerie processed the news. "Well, that's wonderful," she finally said.

Emily noticed the slight delay; she was aware of her mother's concerns. "Mom, it's the prom. I worked hard all these years. This is a celebration of that. I deserve to relax and be happy for the prom."

"Of course, of course," Valerie said, reaching for her cigarettes. "And you'll need a beautiful dress, I suppose?"

"That's right," Emily replied, now embarrassed. "I wanted to ask you about that."

"I'll sew you the most beautiful dress that anyone at your school has ever seen!" her mother reassured her. "You know you can always count on me to take care of you."

Emily sighed, feeling a tremendous burden lift from her shoulders. "Thank you," she whispered and hugged Valerie.

Valerie stepped away from the embrace to light her cigarette. "Now, go do your homework before I change my mind," she said playfully. "Don't think too much about this. You'll have a beautiful dress, and you'll be the most beautiful girl at the dance. But stay focused on your studies. You don't want to lose your momentum before you start college."

"Of course!" Emily left the room with her head down, suppressing a smile of joy.

She was going to have a dress for the prom. It would be the most beautiful one in the school; her mother had promised. As she lay on her bed, Emily felt like her heart was about to burst with happiness. She grabbed one of her pillows, brought it to her chest, and kissed it, imagining it was Robert. She felt like a thirteen-year-old, emotionally and experientially. While all her friends had experienced crushes over these years, she had steered clear of such situations. Now, at the age of seventeen, she was there, on her bed, kissing a pillow, in love and feeling butterflies in her stomach. She was happy.

Emily smiled, stared at the ceiling, found for the small imperfection in the paint above her head, and began to count. "One, two, three, four . . ."

* * *

A few weeks later, May 26, the day of the prom, dawned sunny and warm, unlike the endless days of rain the previous week. The night before, Emily had slept little due to excitement and nervousness. In the past few days, Valerie had taken her measurements several times while working on her dress, but she had refused to show Emily the progress. Her mother wanted it to be a surprise. This had made the young woman even more anxious, and her anxiety grew with each passing day leading up to the event.

It was Saturday, and she wouldn't see Robert until he showed up that evening to escort her to the event. Emily, still weary, went to the kitchen and found Valerie had the dress ready for her, hanging on the display cabinet in the back of the room.

Emily froze, mouth agape, wide-eyed to behold the most magnificent dress she had ever seen. It was pink, her favorite color, and long, strapless, and snug at the waist, flowing down into a skirt made of clouds of satin and rhinestones sewn together to form a pink sky full of stars.

Emily placed her hands over her chest, and tears welled up in her eyes as she heard her mother approach from behind. She felt her mother's hand come to rest on her shoulder. Emily lifted the dress, turned, and hugged her mother more tightly than she had ever done before.

"Do you like it?" Valerie asked.

"It's beautiful, Mom. It's perfect," Emily replied before bursting into tears.

"Good. Now try it on. Let's see if I'm still good at taking measurements," Valerie said with a touch of irony.

"Of course, you are!" the girl replied, smiling, tasting tears on her lips.

The dress fit Emily perfectly, and according to her mother's careful observations, there were no adjustments needed. As the girl looked at herself in the full-length mirror in her mother's workroom, her thoughts turned to Robert. To how they would look together. To how the young man would react when he saw her dressed in that gown.

She smiled.

"I'm sure the boy will love it," Valerie said, as if she had read her daughter's thoughts.

"I'm sure too," Emily replied without taking her eyes off the mirror, twirling the dress from side to side. She caught a glint of mischief in the eyes of her reflection. "I'm quite sure."

* * *

The evening arrived. By six o'clock, Emily had been ready for almost an hour. Valerie had helped her daughter dress and put on makeup, and Emily had been primping in front of the upstairs bathroom mirror for hours, either because she liked what she saw and or because she was trying to figure out if the boy would like it.

Emily was applying a few drops of her mother's Chanel to her wrist when the doorbell rang. Emily jumped, a grin of delight on her face, but Valerie waved for her to stay put and hurried down to open the door for Robert.

It was the first time the woman had seen the boy in person. Robert wore a black suit over a white shirt and a bowtie. Her daughter had been right; he was very handsome, but not just because of his blond hair and green eyes. It was his gaze and his smile that were magnetic. He had a face that showed a kind and lively soul.

That sight almost scared Valerie. She had feared her daughter's feelings for this handsome, intelligent, and charismatic young man would not easily fade with the end of high school. Had Emily been naive to think of it that way, Valerie wondered, or had she just lied to herself and her mother?

"Hello, Mrs. Barton," the young man said kindly. In one hand, he held a box containing a pink corsage, a traditional prom favor, meant for Emily's wrist, in the other, a bouquet of flowers.

"Hello. You must be Robert," Valerie replied.

"Pleasure to meet you, ma'am," the young man responded, his tone slightly embarrassed. "These are for you." He handed her the bouquet.

Valerie was taken aback. "Oh, thank you," she stammered.

At that moment, Robert's gaze passed over Valerie's shoulder. Valerie turned to see Emily gracefully descending the stairs. Emily held a pink boutonniere in her hand, intended for Robert's jacket lapel. She was smiling and visibly excited. Valerie looked at the boy again through narrowed eyes. He seemed hypnotized by the sight of her daughter.

Valerie stepped aside, allowing Robert to enter the house and wait for Emily, who, due to the bulk of her dress, descended very slowly. Once at the foot of the stairs, the two young people exchanged the flowers.

"You look beautiful, Emily Barton," the boy whispered.

"You look handsome, Robert Smith," she replied.

Valerie felt a shiver run down her spine as she realized how deeply in love the two of them were. Taken and infatuated with each other. It was the first time she had seen them together, and now she understood how strong their bond was. She turned away momentarily to place the bouquet on the coffee table.

Robert offered Emily his arm and escorted her out of the house to where a limousine, arranged for by his father just for that important moment, awaited them. Valerie followed. Once outside the door, Robert asked Valerie to take a their photo with his camera. She complied and took several photos.

As she snapped the photos, through the camera's viewfinder, Valerie studied her daughter's excited smile, Robert's proud gaze, and their hands tightly clasped. Emily approached the luxurious car and turned back to her mother, smiling happily. Robert helped her into the car and followed. Valerie handed him the camera, and the driver closed the door behind them, hiding them behind the tinted windows.

Valerie returned inside the house. Almost robotically, she took a glass vase from the kitchen, filled it with water, and went back to the living room to put Robert's flowers in water. She arranged them so that all the blooms had room and sat on the couch. Then she hit play on that day's drama.

* * *

On the short drive to the school, the two young lovers kissed and whispered words of love to each other. Upon arrival, the driver helped them out of the car, and they walked hand in hand toward the entrance of the gym.

Inside, Emily felt as if all eyes had turned to them. She knew they made a stunning couple, both elegant and happy. Within a minute, they were swarmed by Emily's three friends and their respective dates.

The gym had been decked out as it had been for every prom, and the first few hours of the evening passed with laughter, some secret drinks, and a couple of cigarettes smoked outside the venue. Everyone was happy. The prom was the most anticipated event for every student since their first year of high school. It marked the end of their high school journey before graduation and solidified the friendships they had formed within those walls over the previous four years, friendships that would often end and be interrupted forever as everyone went their separate ways to different cities, universities, and pursuits.

For Robert and Emily, their friendship, their love, was one of those relationships that would be severed, perhaps forever. Emily wasn't on social media; her computer and email were strictly for school use, and it had been that way for so long that she didn't anticipate having a long-distance, online relationship with Robert. They would be thousands of miles apart, and in the best-case scenario, they would meet again years later at their ten-year class reunion, each with their own lives, new loves, and careers. That evening, they focused only on the present, as they had been doing for months. There was no need to make any plans for the future, at least not tonight.

Toward the end of the evening, it was time for the traditional crowning of the prom king and queen. The coronation ceremony was met with great enthusiasm by all the students. Typically, the most popular and beloved girl in school was named queen, and almost always, the king was one of the football or basketball players. Every girl's dream, from their first year of school, was to one day become prom queen. The student council president climbed onto the stage, took the microphone, and delivered a brief speech before announcing who had been chosen for these two symbolic titles that year.

All the graduating students had their eyes fixed on the stage. Robert and Emily stood hand in hand, making guesses and comments amidst laughter about who the winners might be.

The student council president opened the envelope to announce the school's prom king for the 2011/2012 school year. He straightened the card inside and jubilantly shouted the name of the chosen one into the microphone, "Robert Smith!"

All the students turned to the back of the room where Emily and Robert were standing, stunned. Mouths agape at the unexpected nomination, the two turned toward each other simultaneously. Emily grinned, took Robert's face in her hands, and kissed him.

"Congratulations, Robert," she whispered. "You deserve it."

At that moment, Robert's friends grabbed him by the arms and dragged him toward the stage, whooping and jumping for joy. Robert climbed the four steps and stood in front of the council president, who crowned him as tradition dictated.

Then, the young presenter returned to the microphone to announce who had been chosen as the prom queen. All of Emily's friends gathered around her.

"I bet it's you, Sandy!" Clare whispered, holding her tightly. "It's the most obvious and well-deserved ending, my friend."

"Who would have thought?" exclaimed Jessica, gripping her hand. "Sandy Barton, prom queen!"

The president pulled out the second card from the envelope, looked around the room, and smiled. "Emily Barton!" he shouted, tossing the two cards into the crowd.

There was a moment of silence in the room, obliterated a few seconds later by Emily's friends' screams as they almost dragged her toward the stage. Emily let herself be pulled, incredulous at the recognition. She slowly ascended the stage to where Robert was waiting, extending his hand with a smile. The young man held her tightly and kissed her gently.

"I love you, my queen," Robert whispered in her ear.

"I love you too, Robert," Emily replied, realizing for the first time just how strong her feelings were for him. She looked into his eyes for a long moment as a second realization swept over her: she would soon have to let go of that love, forever.

Robert steered Emily to the center of the stage, where the student council president crowned her in front of the entire audience. Her three friends were all in tears at the edge of the stage.

Emily's cheeks ached from smiling, and she saw everything as if through a haze. In that moment, she felt as if she was floating between the dream and the nightmare that everything would soon end.

"And now, prom king and queen, make your way to the center of the room. It's time for the dance!" the president shouted.

Robert and Emily descended from the stage, each wearing a crown, and took their place under the spotlight in the center of the room. They looked at each other, hand in hand, as the first notes of Coldplay's "Fix You" began to fill the room. It had been Robert's request for their dance.

Hearing the words of that song, Emily felt a sad tear roll down her cheek. Her thoughts began to drift through all the moments she had shared with Robert.

Fix you, she thought. It was as if he knew the darkness she had lived in and promised to heal her. But he had already done that. He had opened her heart. He had ignited emotions within her that she hadn't known she could feel, emotions she believed her life, her mother, her differences, her mental state, and her cruel destiny had denied her–growing up without a father, without answers and without any questions to ask.

She thought about the future, for the first time, in a different way. For the first time, she saw and dreamed and lived and succeeded with Robert still in the picture. *But how?* she wondered.

"Tonight, I want to be with you," Emily whispered in the boy's ear.

Robert gazed down at her and smiled softly. "Me too, Einstein. Me too."

Emily rested her head on his chest and began to count in a whisper. "One, two, three, four, five . . ."

* * *

Late in the evening, the limousine pulled into Emily's driveway. The driver hurried to open the rear door, and first Emily, then Robert emerged, a little wobbly from the drinks they'd snuck and giggling at the events of the evening. They stood there in front of the car, facing each other, holding hands in the glow of the headlights.

"Would you like to come to my room?" Emily asked.

Robert looked surprised. "What about your mother?"

"She's probably sleeping, and her room is on the main floor. I'll go inside and head to my room. There's a trellis that reaches up to my window," Emily replied, pointing to the upstairs window. "I'll go in, say goodnight to my mom, then I'll signal you from the window, and you can come up."

"Are you sure we won't get into trouble?"

"My room is on the opposite side from my mom's," she whispered, brushing her lips against the boy's neck. "Let's be quiet, and she won't notice anything."

Robert smiled. "Okay. What's the signal?"

"I'll toss my corsage out of the window once it's clear."

"Okay, perfect. I'll tell the driver to leave. I'll have to walk home afterward," the boy concluded with a mischievous grin.

Emily turned and headed toward the house entrance as Robert made his way to the limo.

Emily entered the house and tiptoed to her mother's bedroom. To her surprise, Valerie was still awake.

"How was the evening?" Valerie asked when she saw her daughter in her bedroom doorway.

"It was wonderful, Mom. I was named prom queen!" Emily replied, pretending to yawn.

"Prom queen, hmmm?" Valerie murmured before brightening up. "Well, good for you, Emily."

"Yes, Mom. It was amazing!" Emily said, only partly registering her mother's lack of enthusiasm. "But I'm *really* tired. I'm going to go up to bed." Emily let her arms hang limp at her sides to show just how tired she was.

"Okay, honey. Go ahead. Sleep well. You can tell me all about it tomorrow."

Emily headed for the door, pausing on the threshold and turning back to look at her mother. "Mom . . ."

Valerie paused reaching for the light switch to her bedside lamp. "Yes?"

"I'm head over heels in love with Robert Smith," Emily whispered before fleeing into the hallway.

Emily hurried upstairs and went to the bathroom. She heard a door slam, figuring she'd forgotten to close her mother's door when she left her bedroom. She stayed in the bathroom for a few moments, just listening. Silence had descended upon the house.

Emily slowly emerged from the bathroom and tiptoed into her bedroom. She closed the door slowly, trying not to make any noise. Excitement and adrenaline gave her a shiver. She approached the window cautiously and looked outside. She couldn't see Robert, but she knew he was there waiting for her signal, so she opened the window slightly and dropped her corsage into the darkness below.

She tiptoed back to sit at the head of the bed, facing the window, and waited. She was nervous, so after a minute, she moved to the foot of the bed. She took off her shoes and waited some more.

Five minutes passed in silence, and Robert had not yet appeared at the window. She heard a noise from outside and rose from her seat to open the window and lean out.

She didn't see anyone.

She returned to her bed, her heart now beating rapidly with anxiety. She wondered why Robert had not come up yet. Perhaps he hadn't seen the corsage fall. *Maybe it's too dark for him to notice the signal,* she thought.

Emily began to regret the crazy idea of inviting him up to her room. What had come over her? She got up and went back to the window. Nothing. Silence. Darkness.

She returned to her bed, lay down, and began to count. She did so almost compulsively, feeling a terrible sense of unease.

"One, two, three, four . . ."

A tear rolled down her face, and her crown tumbled from her head and onto the floor. After a few minutes, she fell asleep, still dressed in her pink gown.

Chapter 9

Emily was awakened by the slamming of the front door. She opened her eyes and realized she had fallen asleep on the bed without undressing, washing her face, or removing her makeup.

She looked blearily around. Robert hadn't come, and she wondered why. *He must not have seen the corsage,* she thought. She was sure of it. He'd probably assumed that Emily had changed her mind and walked home after a while. She felt guilty. He had sent the driver away to be with her, and she'd screwed up the signal.

Emily stood, feeling dizzy. It was then that she realized she had drunk quite a bit the night before. It was the first time she had woken up with a hangover. She touched her tender head and went downstairs. She descended the stairs carefully, squinting due to her headache. She felt lightheaded, and when she reached the last step, she tripped over her mother's gardening boots and tumbled to the floor.

Emily winced as pain shot through her right ankle. She was trying to get up when Valerie rushed in from the kitchen.

"What happened, honey?" her mother exclaimed.

"I tripped. It's nothing," Emily replied as she tried to make her way into the kitchen, hopping on one foot.

"Come, sit down. I'll put some ice on your ankle," Valerie said as she opened the fridge and took out an ice pack.

Valerie knelt in front of her daughter, lifting the hem of the pink prom dress.

"It's covered in mud," Valerie chided. "How did you manage to get the dress so dirty? Oh well, never mind. Lift your leg. Let's apply the ice to your ankle."

Emily felt like the room was spinning around her. " I have a terrible headache," she muttered as she massaged her temples.

Valerie scrunched her face. "It must have been all those non-alcoholic punches you had last night," she said sarcastically.

Emily pretended not to hear and didn't reply.

"Honey, I had a prom too, back in my days," her mother continued, shaking her head while trying to secure the ice pack to Emily's ankle. "And even then, we used to drink secretly."

The morning crawled toward half-past nine, and Emily was still sitting with her right leg stretched out on a chair in the kitchen when the doorbell rang.

Valerie went to answer it. Emily leaned back to peek around the doorframe as her mother opened the door to find a worried-looking blond woman with big green eyes.

"Hello. Can I help you?" Valerie asked.

The woman, standing on the doorstep, clutched her hands to her chest. She spoke with an English accent. "Hello, sorry for the disturbance," she blurted. "I'm Robert Smith's mother. My son didn't come home last night after the prom. The limousine driver called us this morning to say that Robert had left his phone in the back seat and had asked to be dropped off here last night. Is he still here?"

Emily stiffened.

Valerie shook her head. "No, ma'am. He's not here."

"Is Emily at home? Can I talk to her?" the woman asked again.

Emily jumped up from her chair and limped to the door. Valerie made way for her at the entrance. "Mrs. Smith!

Has something happened to Robert?" the young woman asked, her voice filled with terror.

Mrs. Smith wore a pained expression. "I don't know! He didn't come back last night. Do you know anything? He would never stay out all night without letting us know."

Emily covered her mouth, then said. "No, ma'am. I don't know anything. He brought me here, and then . . ." Emily paused. She didn't want the mother to hear how they'd planned for night to end.

"Then what, Emily?" Mrs. Smith asked, her now-narrowed eyes scanning Emily's muddied dress and swollen ankle.

There were a few seconds of silence. Emily looked at her mother first and then back at Mrs. Smith. "Then Robert asked the driver to leave because I had invited him inside. To my room. We both had been drinking." Emily looked at her mother as if seeking understanding, but Valerie just looked shocked and irritated. "But Robert never arrived, and I fell asleep," Emily concluded, lowering her gaze toward the floor.

"And he didn't come home!" Robert's mother almost shouted before breaking down in tears of despair. "Where is he? What happened to him?"

"I'm sure there's an explanation for all of this," Valerie said, trying to reassure the woman.

Emily's thoughts, however, immediately turned dark. She agreed with Robert's mother; Robert, for some reason, had disappeared. And that thought sent a shiver down her spine. For a moment, she entertained the idea she was responsible for his disappearance, as had often been the case with things she cared about. But she forcefully pushed that ridiculous thought out of her mind, shaking her head visibly without realizing it.

Valerie seemed to notice the gesture and placed a comforting hand on her daughter's back.

Mrs. Smith turned toward her car, where a man, presumably Robert's father, sat in the driver's seat, talking on his cellphone. Emily assumed he was calling all Roberts friends in the hope of finding him in someone's company. Emily prayed he would be successful.

"Thank you. If Robert shows up, please, Emily, let me know right away," the woman concluded before turning back to her car.

* * *

Emily hobbled up the stairs on her aching ankle, collapsed onto her bed, and burst into tears. With her face buried in the pillow, she began counting quietly, contemplating with increasing worry what could have happened to Robert. "One, two, three, four . . ."

The night before, they were supposed to make love. Her first time. She'd wanted it to be Robert, wanted it to be that night, but he hadn't shown up. And he hadn't gone home. And no one knew where he was.

After nearly two hours, Emily got up and slowly removed the pink dress. She put on a pair of jeans and a Yale logoed T-shirt and went back downstairs. Her ankle hurt less, but there was still pain when she flexed her foot.

Valerie was preparing lunch.

"Mom."

The woman turned and fixed her daughter with a serious look. "Tell me, Emily."

She began tentatively, "About the story with Robert coming over—"

"Let's not talk about it anymore, Emily," Valerie interrupted. "You had a bit too much to drink, and you both thought of doing something foolish. I'm glad he didn't come."

"Do you think something bad happened to him?" Emily asked, more in search of comfort than a real answer.

Valerie lowered her gaze. "I don't know. If it's true that he's not one to stay out all night without telling his parents, then I understand Mrs. Smith's concern." She approached her daughter to hug her. "But we have to stay positive. Let's hope it's just a prom night prank, something kids often do."

Emily nodded. She wanted to believe that was what had happened, despite her terrible unease.

The kitchen phone rang. Emily pulled away from her mother and rushed to answer it.

"Hello! Robert?" the young woman answered.

There were a few seconds of silence.

"No, Emily. It's Jessica."

"Jessica! Hi. Sorry, I was hoping it was Robert," Emily replied.

"I know. I heard. My dad told me the Smiths went to the police station to report his disappearance. *What* happened last night?" Jessica's father was an officer with the Groton Police, which covered Mystic in its jurisdiction.

Emily brought her hand to her mouth, terrified.

"I don't know. He brought me home, and . . ." Emily stopped, just as she had in front of her mother and Mrs. Smith, embarrassed about the whole situation.

"And what?" Jessica pressed.

"Robert and I had decided to go to my room after the prom," Emily whispered. "I went inside while he sent the driver away. I tossed my corsage out the window as soon as the coast was clear, as a signal, but Robert didn't come, and I fell asleep shortly after."

"I don't understand. Robert was supposed to come to your room and didn't show up?" Jessica repeated.

"Exactly," Emily replied, her voice shaky. "Maybe he didn't see the signal and left. I don't know what to think. I'm really worried."

There was another moment of silence.

"My dad told the Smiths," Jessica began, "that even though it hasn't been enough hours for the police to start a search operation, he would activate search dogs right away. He doesn't want to waste time. The Smiths don't believe Robert left on his own."

"I don't believe it either," Emily cried.

"We'll find him," Jessica said with a note of forced positivity in her voice.

* * *

Not even two hours had passed since Emily had spoken on the phone with her friend when the dark blue vans of the police search dog unit arrived outside her house. Three vans pulled up, and four men got out. The officers opened the rear doors of the vans, and each released a dog. Behind them, from a Groton Police car, a short, slender man with graying hair stepped out, followed by another man, taller and younger than the first with brown hair and bushy eyebrows. They strode to the entrance, and the detective knocked vigorously.

Emily opened the door. "Can I help you?" Emily asked.

"Hello, I'm Detective White," said the short man, flashing a detective's badge, "and this is my partner, Frank Avellino. You must be Emily," the man said.

"Yes, I'm Emily," the girl replied apprehensively. "Have you found Robert?"

"No, miss," said the detective, his voice sorrowful. "But we're looking for him. That's why we're here. We would like to talk to you for a few minutes, if you don't mind."

"Of course," Emily replied, stepping outside the house to observe the group of officers preparing for the search with the dogs.

"Mrs. Smith told us that you and Robert went to the prom together last night. Is that correct?" Detective White asked.

"Yes, as I told Mrs. Smith this morning, after the prom, we came here to my house. We had decided to have some private time in my room, so Robert sent the limo away. But after I went upstairs, he didn't come up."

"Explain further," White pressed. "What do you mean he didn't come up?"

Emily shifted her gaze to the sky. It was the third time she had to recount this embarrassing story. "It means that I was supposed to make sure my mom was in bed first. Then I was supposed to go to my room and toss my corsage out of the window. That was the signal that the coast was clear for him to climb up the trellis below my window." She gestured toward the planter box and trellis under her window.

White followed the gesture and then raised his eyes. "And did you do that?"

"Yes. After saying goodnight to my mom, I went to my room. I waited for a few minutes, and then I opened the window. I didn't see Robert, but I assumed he was out here. So, I dropped my corsage down. But he didn't come up. After waiting for a while, I fell asleep on the bed, still in my prom dress." As she concluded, a sudden realization struck her.

"What's wrong, Emily?" Detective White asked, noticing the girl's confused and questioning gaze.

Emily didn't take her eyes off that corner of the house right under her window. "If Robert didn't see my signal," Emily whispered, "the corsage should still be out here."

Feeling the detective's eyes watching her every move, Emily hobbled toward the trellis and scanned the area, then limped to the closed garage door, then back to below the window, and finally behind the corner of the house. Nothing. "It should be around here somewhere."

"What, Emily?" Detective White asked.

"The corsage!" she replied, as if he should have asked that question before her. "I thought Robert didn't come up to my room because he didn't see my corsage drop from the window. So, it should be around here."

She turned just in time to see Detective White casting a narrow-eyed glance at his partner. "Emily, do you have any suspicion about where Robert might have gone?" the detective asked, falling into step behind her.

"No, Detective. I don't know what to think. If Robert found the corsage, he would have come up."

White gave her a comforting smile. "We will do everything to find him, Emily. Don't worry. Can I speak with your mother?"

"Yes, she's inside."

Emily followed the detective back to the front door, where they found Valerie standing on the threshold, observing the scene.

"Mrs. Barton," White said, "we should let the dogs enter your property to help them pick up any traces of Robert's presence.

"Of course, Detective, go ahead," the woman replied.

"In the meantime," White asked, "can you tell me anything about last night? Where were you when your daughter came home?"

"I was in bed," Valerie replied, her arms crossed. "That's where Emily found me when she came home. And I stayed there until this morning."

White turned to the officers waiting at the end of the driveway and waved for them to begin the search. Emily moved to stand beside her mother, watching as the four policemen bent down to let the dogs sniff a T-shirt belonging to Robert, then immediately released them. The German shepherds began sniffing around the property, pausing one by one between the corner under Emily's window and the garage before turning toward the outer edge of the property. They had only gone about a hundred feet before they stopped again, forming a circle around a point.

Nothing else.

One of the officers approached Detective White. "Stern, what's going on?" the detective asked.

"The dogs found a trace," Stern replied with a disappointed look, pointing to a spot outside the property. "The young man was here, but he must have driven away because the dogs lost his scent not far from here."

White didn't respond, staring at the spot the dogs had identified with a contemplative look on his face. "Emily!" he called suddenly, turning to the girl.

Emily startled. "Yes, Detective."

"I'd like to ask you some more questions, but at the police station," he continued, then turned to Valerie. "Ma'am, since your daughter is a minor, I'd like you to come as well."

"Certainly," they both replied, almost in unison.

* * *

Mrs. Barton and her daughter entered the Groton Police Station less than an hour later and were shown into a small meeting room to spare Emily the tension of the interrogation room. Once informed of their arrival, Detective White picked up the phone and dialed Frank Avellino's extension. "Frank, the girl is here with her mother. I'm going to ask her some questions. In the meantime, get a search warrant for the house. Just to be safe."

"What are you thinking, Tony?" Avellino asked, audibly confused.

"I don't know, Frank," White replied, tapping his finger on the desktop. "The girl seems sincere, but she's a bit peculiar. There's something off about this whole story. I want to get to the bottom of it, and I believe we should start with her and that house."

"Okay, boss," Avellino concluded.

Hanging up the phone, Detective White got up and headed to the meeting room. Emily was waiting in a chair, with Valerie sat on a small couch. White sat across from Emily and placed a small tape recorder on the table. He smiled at her, and she returned the gesture.

"So, Emily, let's start from the beginning." He turned on the recorder. "What was your relationship with Robert like?"

Emily lowered her gaze to the table and stared at it for a moment before responding, "Robert and I were dating. Initially, we were only in a few classes together, especially chemistry, and we sat close to each other. After a while, he gave me a gift, and I returned the favor. We kissed, and from that point on, we became a steady couple. All of this happened only in the last year because Robert only moved to Mystic twelve months ago."

"What happened on the night of the prom?" White asked. "Do you remember anything strange or unusual?"

"Nothing strange. Robert came to pick me up in a limousine, and we went to the prom together. We had a lot of fun, snuck some drinks with some classmates outside the gym, and in the end, he was named prom king, and I was prom queen. We were have a great time. We danced and then came back home. I asked him to come up to my room. We were both a bit tipsy and excited about the evening. He agreed and sent the limousine away."

"And then? What happened?" Detective White pressed.

Emily's voice trembled. "And then I told him to wait below my window. I was supposed to go inside alone and make sure my mom was in bed, which she was. I went to the bathroom and then to my room. The signal was my corsage. If I dropped it from the window, it meant he could climb up the trellis."

"But Robert didn't come up," White added.

Emily lowered her gaze, remembering her disappointment. "No. I dropped my corsage from the window and sat on the bed, waiting. I had left the window slightly open, expecting him. But after a while, maybe because of the alcohol,

I fell asleep and woke up the next morning, still in my prom dress."

There were a few seconds of silence before the detective shifted his gaze to Emily's mother. "Mrs. Barton, how long have you known Robert?"

The woman, taken aback, cleared her throat and straightened up on the couch. "I met Robert for the first time yesterday evening," she replied confidently. "I knew who he was and that he was dating my daughter, but I had never met him before."

"And when Emily came home, were you in bed?" White added.

"Yes, Detective. Exactly."

"And you didn't leave your bed afterward?"

"Exactly," Valerie replied.

White turned his attention back to Emily. "Emily," the detective asked gingerly, "have you had any contact with your father since he separated from your mother?"

"And how does this have anything to do with Robert, Detective?" Valerie asked irritably.

"I apologize, ma'am, if I was less than delicate," White replied kindly, glancing at Mrs. Barton. "But I'm trying to piece together the situation, including the family dynamics. In cases like this, I'm used to leaving no stone unturned."

"My father didn't separate from my mother," Emily interjected firmly, locking eyes with the detective. "He abandoned us eleven years ago and never returned. I haven't seen or heard from him since."

There were a few more seconds of silence. "I'm sorry, Emily," White replied, lowering his head toward the recorder. "Going back to last night, are you sure you didn't notice anything unusual? Anyone Robert might have had an argument with or disagreements of any kind during the prom?"

"No, Detective," the girl replied. "Nothing. We never left each other's side except to go to the bathroom. We had a great time all evening. Jessica, Mary, Clare, and their dates were with us, and we had a lot of fun."

At that moment, Detective Avellino entered the room and gave a thumbs-up. It was the sign White had been waiting for; his partner had received clearance for the search of the Barton's house. White turned his gaze back to the young woman, staring at her for a while before shifting his focus to her mother.

"Mrs. Barton, why have you never met Robert before the prom?" Detective White asked, intrigued. "The young man had been dating your daughter for many months, and he had never been over to your house, perhaps for studying or just for dinner?"

Valerie stiffened without responding. It was Emily who spoke up, "Detective, that was my choice. Robert and I didn't see each other outside of school and school functions. I take my studies very seriously. I wanted us both to maintain our grade-point averages, and I study alone. I always have." She stared sadly at the table separating her from White.

Frank Avellino reappeared at the door. "Detective, may I have a word?" he asked, clearly out of breath. "It's urgent."

Avellino's grim expression didn't bode well. White got up, apologized to Emily and her mother, and followed Avellino into the corridor.

"What's going on, Frank?" White asked.

Avellino shuddered as he delivered the news: "They found a body of a young man in an old, disused water cistern near the river."

"Murdered?" White inquired.

"I don't know yet. As soon as I got the call, I rushed here to tell you."

"Who found the body?"

"It seems to have been a man out jogging," Avellino replied.

"Okay. You go ahead. I'll wrap things up with the girl for now and join you," the detective concluded.

White returned to the room where the Bartons were waiting. He sat down, trying to find the right words to deliver the news he had just received. Even though he had had to do it before, it was never easy to inform relatives or friends that their loved one, who had gone missing, had been found, but not alive.

It hadn't been confirmed yet that it was Robert, but this was Mystic. One of the safest towns in America. And it had been years since a murder had occurred in the area. It couldn't be a coincidence.

After a few seconds of sitting in silence with his head bowed, Detective White finally looked at the girl. "Emily," he said, almost in a whisper, "my partner just informed me that a body was found near the river not long ago. We don't know for sure if it's Robert, but . . ." He let his words trail off. He didn't bother saying that it likely was.

Emily's sea-green eyes filled with tears. She buried her face in her hands and sobbed. Valerie's eyes widened in shock, and then she suddenly rose and embraced her daughter from behind, gently stroking her head as if to comfort and reassure her. White watched the mother and daughter with interest and pity.

Chapter 10

By the time Anthony White arrived at the scene where the body had been discovered, the forensics team, a fire engine, an ambulance, Detective Avellino, and four other police officers were already present.

Detective White parked along River Road. Just below the roadside, a several feet down, he could see the abandoned cistern. He stepped out of the car and scanned the area, first looking down the embankment and then back at his vehicle, then gazing across to the other side of the river toward the historic Elm Grove Cemetery and then back down the road from which he had come.

"Detective!" Avellino called in the distance, raising his arm to get his partner's attention.

White acknowledged with a nod and made his way toward a small trail that led to the cistern, carefully avoiding puddles left by the recent days' rain. The cistern was a concrete tank nearly eight feet in diameter and protruding about three feet above the ground, plunging down more than twelve feet deep on the inside.

"What can you tell me, Frank?" he asked, out of breath, peering at the concrete tank.

"The guy who found the body is sitting there," Avellino said, pointing to a middle-aged man dressed in shorts and a T-shirt from the previous year Boston Marathon.

"We'll get to him in a moment," White replied, peering down into the gloom of the cistern. "What can you tell me about the body?"

"I made them wait for you," Avellino replied. "The forensic team says they need to lift it first before examining the cistern."

"I understand. Okay. Let them lift the body. Let's see who it is."

Avellino signaled for the forensic team to begin.

It took almost an hour to complete the retrieval operation. In the meantime, White seated himself on a rock beside the man dressed in jogging attire, who still appeared disturbed by the discovery.

"Hello, I'm Detective White. What's your name, sir?" the detective asked.

"I'm Jerry Stone," replied the man, his gaze still fixed on the cistern.

"Please tell me everything. Leave out no details."

Jerry bowed his head, as if searching the ground for pieces of his memory. "Like almost every morning, I come here to run along the river. It's about eight miles every day. I participate in many marathons; it's my passion. Today, though, when I got near this cistern, I noticed my shoelaces were untied. So, I stopped, put my foot up on the cistern to tie them. I don't know why or what made me do it, but I looked inside. I saw something that looked like a person. Out of instinct, I jumped back, but then I took a closer look. I shone my cellphone light inside and saw that it was a body. Lifeless, I assumed. So I called 911 right away."

"Anything else, Jerry?" Detective White urged. "Did you see anyone during your run? Any cars parked on the street?"

"No, nothing else. This place is deserted in the morning. That's why I come here for my run," Jerry concluded.

At that moment, Avellino gestured for his superior to come closer. The lifeless body found in the cistern had been brought to the surface. It was that of a young man, dressed in formal attire, with blond hair.

It was Robert Smith.

The body was placed on a plastic sheet not far from the cistern, and the forensic team began to examine it delicately.

"Do you think he fell in?" Avellino asked, standing next to White and watching the operation.

"Anything's possible. But what was he doing here? The Barton house is southwest from here, and the Smith home is southeast. Why did the body come here, and at that hour of the night?"

Avellino grimaced. "Maybe he wanted to take a walk to sober up. He was probably disoriented. Who knows? When it comes to prom night, young folks do the strangest things. Alcohol, drugs . . ." The deputy detective shook his head.

At that moment, the head of the forensic team signaled for the two detectives to approach. "Detective, take a look here," the man said, leaning over Robert's body and pointing at a spot beneath his nape. "I don't want to speculate before the autopsy, but I believe the victim was stabbed from behind, right under the nape. And judging by the wound and its position, I think it was a fatal blow. It's right at the spinal process. There's also a lot of bruises, but no sign of struggle, so those probably came from being dumped in the cistern."

White turned to his deputy. "I think, at this point, we can rule out accidental falling," he said.

White approached the body. Robert's eyes were closed, his body curled in a fetal position. His hair was tangled with dry leaves and stained with blood, and he only had one shoe on.

"Okay. Let me know when you have the autopsy results and when you've examined the cistern and the area," White ordered as he turned to climb the path back to his car. "Tell me if you find anything interesting."

"Okay, Detective," answered one of the forensic officers.

"By the way," White continued, turning back toward the cistern, "let me know if you find a corsage."

"Of course, Detective."

White and Avellino paused in front of their cars to reflect.

"What do you think, Tony?" his deputy asked.

"Well, excluding the possibility of a fall or suicide," White replied, pointing to the spot above the cistern's opening, from which the body could have been easily dropped, "it's clear that the young man was murdered. From behind, in cold blood. I don't think it happened here. He was killed somewhere else, and his lifeless body was brought here, clearly in a car. And most likely, but that's where I'd place my bet, the body was thrown down from this point until it fell into the cistern."

Avellino followed the detective's gestures with his eyes. By his stern expression, White knew it seemed like the most plausible scenario to him as well. But in situations like this, every detective spoke in hypotheticals, even when everything seemed quite clear. No detective liked to be wrong about a theory, and experience had taught them anything was possible in that world. Often, what seemed impossible became reality, especially when it came to gruesome murders.

"Okay, I'm heading to the station," White said, unlocking his car and opening the door. "I have more questions for the Bartons. You get ready for the search of their residence.

Let's see if we can find any more clues related to that poor boy. Summon all the boy's friends, especially those who were with the couple during the dance. And do me a favor, find me the girl's father. His name is Albert Barton. And I hate to put this on you but please notify the Smith family. I'll need to question them as well, but let them process for a bit."

Avellino solemnly agreed as he stepped into his car.

* * *

Once at the police station, Detective White returned to the room where Emily had been crying inconsolably for nearly three hours. He sat down in front of the young woman and activated the recorder once again.

"Emily, unfortunately, I have to give you some terrible news," the detective began.

Emily burst into tears once more, and White knew she had already figured it out–that the body found was Robert's. He gave her a few minutes to compose herself before he resumed with the questions.

"First of all, Mrs. Barton," he said briskly, turning to Valerie, "I must inform you that as a matter of procedure, and since the last place Robert was seen was at your house, I've requested a search warrant for your residence."

Valerie's face turned crimson. "What do you mean by a search, Detective?" she demanded, as if the answer wasn't obvious.

"I mean we need to enter your home and conduct investigations to look for possible evidence," Detective White replied calmly.

"As we've already told you," said Valerie, standing and crossing her arms imperiously over her chest, "Robert has never been to our house. There's nothing in that house that could help you in your investigation. And the idea of strangers rummaging through our most intimate belongings is quite disturbing."

Anthony White grimaced. He understood the woman's embarrassment, but he also knew that, especially outside the house, there was a possibility of finding something that could help in the investigation. Experience had taught him not to rule out the possibility that Emily might be hiding something from him.

"I'm sorry, Mrs. Barton, but it's a necessary action, with or without your permission," the man concluded.

Valerie turned toward the door, palpably furious. "Whatever, Detective," she sniped.

"Anything that can lead to finding out who killed my Robert," the trembling-voiced Emily chimed in.

Valerie turned back to the two of them, slumping onto the couch.

"Mrs. Barton," Detective White said firmly, "my officers are outside, ready to escort you home so they can open the door. I wouldn't want to have it forced open. Meanwhile, with your permission, Emily and I could continue our conversation."

"Okay, Detective. I have my car outside, thank you," the woman replied.

"No, ma'am, your car stays here," White replied. "It's included in our warrant for inspection."

Valerie then left the room without saying goodbye, leaving a cloud of fury in her wake. Detective White remained alone with Emily, who by now had buried her face in her hands. The detective could feel the young woman's pain.

"I understand what you're going through right now, Emily. Truly," the man said gently. "You need to gather your strength. You must try to remember everything that happened last night. There must be something from last night that led to Robert ending up killed and left in that cistern."

"Killed?" Emily repeated, visibly confused.

"Yes, Emily. Robert was killed."

"How?"

White took a deep breath before responding, struggling to explain such a gruesome act to a young girl. "His body has a deep puncture wound at the nape. That's all we know so far. But it's at a point that leads us to believe he was fatally stabbed from behind."

Emily remained silent for a moment and then began to gag. The detective pulled a pail over, but she only dry heaved. When she began hyperventilating, White ran out of the room to get help.

* * *

Once they arrived at the Barton's house, Avellino allowed Valerie to unlock the door. However, he requested that she stay outside, under the supervision of one of his officers. Three had been assigned to thoroughly inspect the exterior of the house and the garage, while the detective entered the residence, accompanied by two other colleagues.

On the ground floor, they found nothing unusual. The Luminol they used didn't detect any traces of blood. In the basement, however, they discovered various items packed in boxes or placed on shelves, and a door locked with a padlock. Avellino sent an officer to ask Valerie for the key to unlock it; she's replied that her husband had had the only key and must have taken it with him when he left.

Avellino broke the lock. The space beyond reminded him of the new reality show *American Pickers,* where people hoarded vintage items, mostly junk but some of high value. There was an aging photo on the wall of two little girls, and boxes of assorted sizes lined the shelves. He aimed his flashlight at the cluttered Formica table in the center of the room. Among the various items strewn there, right in the center of the table, he spotted a corsage. "Damn it!" he exclaimed.

He carefully picked it up with tweezers to avoid contamination and inspected it. Spying a small, black drop on one of the petals, he sprayed it with Luminol to check if it was blood.

The drop glowed.

"Bingo!"

Avellino pulled an evidence collection bag from his pocket and placed the corsage inside before returning to the upper floor.

In Emily's room, he found one of the two officers inspecting the dress the young woman had worn to the prom. It was lying across the bed with mud splashes near the hem on one side of the dress. Avellino had it bagged as evidence as well.

Just then, one of the officers inspecting the garage called out to Avellino from below. "Detective! You better come see this!"

Avellino left the room and headed toward the voice. At the foot of the stairs, an officer gestured toward the door leading into the garage.

Avellino followed and found the other officer crouched down, spritzing the concrete the Luminol. The floor displayed a large fluorescent stain about three feet in diameter. Without the aid of the lamp, the floor appeared to have been recently washed and scrubbed with ammonia that still emitted an acrid odor. However, the substance clearly revealed the presence of blood. A forensic photographer snapped a picture of the stain before the Luminol glow could fade.

"This is getting serious. I'm calling White. Be careful where you step. This is now a potential crime scene," Avellino cautioned as he exited the garage with his phone in hand.

His gaze intersected Valerie's. She stood not far away, leaning against one of the police cars, with her arms crossed and a furious expression.

* * *

White snatched up his ringing cell phone and spoke, "White."

"Tony, we've got evidence of foul play at the Barton house," came Avellino's voice from the other end of the line.

"Tell me everything, Frank," White responded, watching Emily closely. A female officer had helped her calm down earlier, and now the girl just sat there, starting at the ceiling and counting quietly.

Avellino described in detail the blood in the garage, the blood-stained corsage discovered in the locked basement room, and Emily's mud-spattered dress.

As Avellino spoke, White peered at Emily, trying to piece together the puzzle. He recalled the puddles at the crime scene.

"Have you checked the truck yet?" the detective interrupted.

"Not yet," Avellino replied. "The truck is still in front of the station. I'll send someone right away."

"Okay. Let me know as soon as possible," White concluded before hanging up.

The detective took a few seconds to reflect. Emily's despair seemed genuine in his view, but something didn't add up. He thought about Avellino's words. Emily's dress had mud on it.

"Emily," he said calmly, "on the phone, my deputy told me they found the corsage you wore last night."

"Where?" Emily asked, her eyes wide with surprise.

"At your house," he replied matter-of-factly. "And they found traces of blood on it."

Emily gasped.

"And they found your dress, too. It has mud on it."

Emily's hands flew to her cheeks. "I knew it. I knew it!" she cried.

"What did you know, Emily?" White asked, leaning forward.

"I knew it!" Emily wailed again. "It was me!"

"What do you mean it was you, Emily?" the detective asked, keeping his calm.

"I don't remember anything, but it was me. Like with everything else," the young woman replied, gazing up at the ceiling with a a mix of anguish and resignation.

"Explain further," White pressed.

"When I was five," she began, "after my father abandoned me, I started making things disappear—toys, trinkets, anything special to me. It's as if they just vanish into thin air, and

I don't remember hiding or throwing them out. I was in therapy for years to learn to cope with this strange condition, and after a while, I guess it worked because things finally stopped disappearing. But then Robert came along. The most special thing to me . . ." She lowered her gaze to the table and started to sob.

"And when Robert came along?" White asked.

There were a few seconds of silence as Emily tried to compose herself. Then she said, "When Robert came along, I began to fear that he might disappear too. But I never imagined I could or would hurt him! I loved him."

White listened to these seemingly nonsensical words, trying to figure out how to proceed. "Try to remember, Emily. Try to remember what happened to Robert. Can you explain why we found mud on your prom dress?"

"I don't know!" the young woman nearly shouted. "I don't remember how I got the dress dirty! I don't remember! I *never* remember!"

"So, you killed him, but you don't remember doing it?" White asked, trying to hide his confusion.

Emily rubbed the back of her neck. "I don't remember. . . . but there's no other logical explanation. I destroy everything beautiful in my life."

White's phone pinged. It was a text from Avellino: "Back at the station. Traces of blood in the pickup truck."

White typed a hasty reply and turned his attention back to Emily. "Do you often drive the pickup truck in your garage?

"What? I've never driven my father's truck . . . or any car," Emily replied, her eyes wide. "I don't have my driver's license yet. We can't afford driving lessons, according to my mother. I was going to start lessons hopefully after graduation."

White squinted, pondering, and at that moment, he saw Avellino approaching through the glass door. "Emily, can you excuse me for just a few minutes?" the detective asked as he got up from his seat.

"Yes, " Emily replied with a broken voice.

"In the meantime, I'll have some snacks and something to drink brought in for you, okay?"

Emily nodded.

White doubted she had any appetite, even though she hadn't eaten anything for hours. He left the room and motioned for his colleague to follow him into the adjacent room. Once inside, he closed the door and turned to Avellino. "The girl sort of confessed to me. She says she killed the boy, but she doesn't remember doing it."

Avellino reacted emphatically, "Nonsense. Let's arrest her."

White grimaced. "I don't know. How could she have transported the body to the cistern? She doesn't have a driver's license, and she says she's never driven a car."

A brief silence ensued as the two investigators contemplated the situation.

"Okay, Tony," Avellino began, "here's how I see it. The girl kills her boyfriend, for who knows what reason. Then she confesses to her mother, who decides to help her get rid of the body. They load the young man's lifeless body into the bed of the pickup truck. She's still wearing her prom dress, and together they dump the body down from River Road into the cistern. She gets mud on her dress in the process. Then they return home, try to clean up the evidence, and hide the corsage in the basement room."

White shook his head. "I don't know. The girl claims she's doesn't remember things. She told me she makes everything she cares about 'disappear into thin air' without any recollection of doing it."

"Well, that could be the motive," Avellino pressed. "She has memory lapses, and that's why she seems sincere. Maybe she really doesn't remember."

"I don't know," White said again, running his hands through his graying hair. "It's a possibility. But let's be cautious. There are still many threads to unravel to discover what really happened." He opened the door to return to Emily. "Bring the girl's mother in. Let's make sure we follow all the proper procedures. I don't want any errors in this case."

"Okay, okay," Avellino said, but just as White was about to leave the room, he grabbed his colleague's arm. "Hang on . . . just thought of something strange that happened earlier at the Barton house." His eyes flew upward as if trying to piece together the details.

"What is it, Frank?" White asked, somewhat impatiently.

"The corsage," Avellino began, "I found it in a small room in the basement, but the door was padlocked. When we asked Mrs. Barton for the key, she said she didn't have it and that her husband probably took it with him when he left. She said she hadn't been in that room since."

White moved fully back into the room. "So, what are you thinking? That the girl had the key all along without her mother knowing?"

With a shrug of his shoulders, Avellino said, "Don't know. You're right . . . there *are* a lot of moving parts to this story. This is a complicated one."

"Speaking of complicated, any updates on finding the father?"

"We're still searching," Avellino replied. "I've got Helen working on it. She's checking various online databases."

The two detectives exchanged a look of concern before White turned and left. Outside the office, he heard shouting in the entrance hall of the police station. He peeked into the hallway to see what was happening.

It was Mrs. Smith, both supported and restrained by her husband. "I want to see that murderer!" she screamed through her tears. "I want to know why! Why did she do it? Why? My child!"

Clearly someone had leaked the news about the bloodstains found at the Barton house, prompting the Smiths to rush to the station in search of answers.

White wanted answers, too. But Emily had said she couldn't provide them. And the detective had the feeling that the girl was sincere; he felt she had been from the beginning. *She was the one to inquire about the corsage,* he thought. *If she remembered killing him, if she had been the one to keep the corsage, then she wouldn't have directed the investigation toward that object.*

He needed to clear things up. It was time to talk to the mother again. He knew that, somehow, the woman must be involved in the whole affair. But he wanted to find out to what extent. Avellino's theory of collaboration between the two, he thought, wasn't entirely implausible.

When White returned to the meeting room, he found Emily and Valerie seated side by side. The mother was once again trying to console her daughter, holding her in an embrace. She looked up at him.

"Mrs. Barton, thank you for your cooperation so far," White began, "but I believe it's time to clarify a series of developments that have emerged at your home and in Emily's account."

"Emily didn't kill anyone," Valerie replied. "She's just confused. She says nonsensical things."

"Indeed, Mrs. Barton. So why don't you help us clear things up?" White asked, staring at the woman with a stern gaze.

* * *

Officer Max Green gritted his teeth as he rappelled down into the damp gloom of the cistern. He landed on his feet in a deep bed of dry leaves that impeded his movements and swept his flashlight beam around the tomblike space. The light immediately caught on the missing shoe belonging to the deceased teenager. The body had already been taken to the coroner's office, and the latest report had confirmed that the boy had already been dead when his body tumbled into the cistern.

Max shivered, treading clumsily in search of more relevant clues, doing his best not to disturb anything despite the unstable ground. It was when he stood up to inspect the wall of the tank that he felt something catch on the tip of his shoe.

He lowered his head while slowly raising his foot, simultaneously trying to point his flashlight at that spot. His white sterile suit and abseiling harness limited his range of motion. He placed his hands against the damp concrete wall and lifted his left foot, bringing it to the surface from under the foliage. When he saw what had attached itself to his foot, he jumped back, striking the concrete wall, and ended up sprawled on the ground.

“Damn it! Damn it!” he yelled, terrified. Raising his eyes from the grisly thing still stuck to his boot, he saw two of his colleagues lean over the tank, silhouetted in the fading light.

“What’s happening, Max?” one shouted, shining a flashlight down toward him. Everything okay down there?”

“Guys, you really need to see this!” Max shouted, all the while keeping his left foot raised. “Call the boss!”

Max beamed his flashlight upward, illuminating the faces of all seven members of the forensics team, all dressed in white sterile suits with masks on their faces. The captain took a small flashlight from his pocket and pointed it toward the bottom of the tank, illuminating Max’s foot and what was, unmistakably, a human skull.

“Get Max out of there!” the captain shouted.

Chapter 11

Emily's heart pounded as White took a seat across from her mother.

"Let's start with the garage," Detective White suggested to Valerie. "Can you explain whose blood is on the floor in the garage and how long it's been there, Mrs. Barton?"

Valerie lowered her gaze to the table, clasping her hands together. "I know nothing about blood in the garage. And I don't know how long it has been there," she replied calmly.

White cleared his throat. "Mrs. Barton, do you know where we found Emily's corsage from the night before?"

"No, Detective," Valerie replied.

"In a basement room. A room locked with a padlock, the key to which, as you told my colleague, you claim to have never had. How do you explain that, Mrs. Barton?"

Emily's eyes widened in surprise. That room had remained locked the whole time her father had been gone.

"I've never had the key to that room, Detective," Valerie replied harshly. "When my husband left us, he must have taken the key with him."

"Emily, did you put the corsage in that room?" the detective asked, snapping his gaze to the young girl.

Emily's confusion deepened. "No. I don't remember. I don't know!"

"You don't remember," said White in a frustrated tone. "You said that. You make things disappear and forget that you've done it."

The detective paused for a moment. When he spoke again, harsh and angry, each sentence landed like a hammer blow on Emily's already fragile nerves. "So, you know what I think about this whole story, Mrs. Barton?" he asked Valerie. "I believe Emily is right. Because of her strange psychological condition, as she herself told me, and for which she had been in therapy for years, she killed Robert. Instead of bringing him upstairs to her room, she convinced him to follow her into the garage. There, at a moment when the boy had his back turned, she stabbed him. In the back of the head. And then, to protect her, you decided to dispose of the body. You loaded it on to the pickup truck, drove to the river, and together, you dumped him into that cistern. You returned home, and you did your best to clean the vehicle and the garage floor. Meanwhile, Emily fell asleep from exhaustion after that long night, and when she woke up in the morning, she didn't remember anything. Just like every time she made things disappear. But this time, what disappeared was an innocent boy with a future ahead of him, taken away in an instant. And for what reason? Who knows."

Emily burst into tears, covering her face with her hands. At that point, it was all clear to her. She had done it again, and this time it had cost her the most beautiful person who had ever entered her life.

"No, Detective," Valerie stated. "Emily didn't kill anyone."

Emily choked on a sob, raising her head to see her mother shake her head, her expression icy.

"Then who killed him, Mrs. Barton?" White asked, clearly impatient.

Her mother remained silent.

"Ma'am," said White, suddenly calm, "I believe it's time for you to ask for a lawyer. It's getting late, and based on what we've discovered and what I consider a confession, I'm obligated to detain Emily until tomorrow when the judge will decide whether to arrest her on murder charges." White glanced at his watch.

"You're making a big mistake, Detective. My daughter didn't kill anyone, and you won't take her away from me!" Valerie was near shouting now. "My daughter isn't going anywhere! She's coming home with me!" Valerie leapt out of her seat, slamming her hand forcefully on the tabletop.

Emily was too stunned to cry anymore.

At that moment, White's phone rang. The detective checked the screen and grimaced. "Excuse me. I have to take this," White said, getting up and leaving the room.

Valerie slumped into her chair and wrapped Emily in her arms. "Honey, stay calm. You didn't do anything. You won't go to prison. I'm here to protect you. I won't let anyone harm you or take you away from me. No one."

Emily heard her mother's words, but they barely registered. Her whole being had gone numb.

* * *

"Tell me, Clark," White barked into the phone as he shut himself in his empty office. "I hope it's important. I'm in the middle of a murder arrest."

"Who are you arresting, Tony?" the man replied.

"Emily Barton, the seventeen-year-old girlfriend of the late Robert Smith," the detective replied, pacing back and forth. "We found blood in the garage and on the corsage she wore last night at the dance. Her dress has mud stains on it. But the most important *clue* is that she confessed. She said she killed the boy but doesn't remember doing it."

Clark cleared his throat. "Well, she doesn't remember doing it because it wasn't her, Tony."

White's pacing ground to a halt. "What do you mean?"

"We found the skeleton of another victim at the bottom of the cistern. And it's been there for at least a decade. Skull crushed. The clothes the victim was wearing are torn from time, but we found the wallet with the documents still intact."

"Whose is it, Clark?" White demanded impatiently.

There were a few seconds of silence.

"It's Albert Barton."

Detective White clenched his fist tightly, then opened it and ran his hand through his hair. Clarity sank in.

Albert Barton hadn't abandoned his family. He had been killed. Eleven years earlier. When Emily Barton was just five years old. He had been murdered and thrown into that cistern. The same cistern where Robert Smith's body had been found eleven years later.

The truth stared him in the face. At this point, his job was only to figure out why.

"What else, Clark?" White asked, impatient to wrap things up and return to the room where Emily and her mother were waiting for him. "Have you found anything else in that damned place?"

"Well, in that cistern, there's a bit of everything. People throw all kinds of trash from the street. Cans, beer bottles, and many other things."

"Okay. Catalog everything. Anything could be crucial to the case," the detective said and then ended the call.

Before leaving the room, White took a series of deep breaths, trying to put his thoughts together. Coincidences didn't exist in his line of work, and this was the most absurd one that could have been imagined. The person responsible for two murders was connected to the Bartons. Or *was* one of the Bartons. And Emily had been only five years old when her father had disappeared.

White returned to Emily and her mother.

"Detective, believe me," Valerie said as soon as he entered the room. "Emily didn't kill anyone. My daughter is devastated. You cannot arrest her."

White took a seat and looked into the woman's eyes. "You're right, Mrs. Barton. Emily didn't kill anyone. Emily is just another victim in all of this." The detective paused, then looked to Emily, who shifted uncomfortably. "Would you do me a favor and leave me and your mother alone for a few minutes?"

Once Emily was settled in the adjacent room under the watch of one of the few officers still at the facility at that hour, White returned to his seat, alone with Valerie.

"So, Mrs. Barton, I believe it's time to tell the truth. We've discovered something that tightens the circle of suspects. And at the center of that circle is you." The detective leaned in toward the woman, elbows on the table.

"Me?" Valerie replied peevishly. "Detective, I was sleeping last night. Emily has already told you she found me in bed when she came back. I was in my pajamas!"

"Why did your husband leave you and vanish without a trace?" White asked calmly.

Valerie hesitated. "We didn't get along. Not for a long time. And one fine morning, I woke up and found a goodbye letter. Nothing else." Valerie lowered her gaze.

"And he never got in touch again? Not even to see Emily?"

"No, Detective. Albert never came back."

"Do you know why, Mrs. Barton?" White asked, narrowing his eyes.

"Why?" Valerie asked, her voice trembling.

"Because Albert, in reality, ended up at the bottom of the same cistern where we found Robert Smith," the detective almost whispered, leaning in to within inches of her face.

* * *

Detective Frank Avellino was in the middle of questioning one of Robert's friends while still monitoring the searches for Emily's father when one of the officers brought him up to speed on the new developments. Avellino immediately went to see Emily.

The girl's face was still marked by earlier tears, and she sat staring vacantly at the wall with her hands clasped between her legs.

Avellino sat across from her and offered a faint smile. "I understand what you're feeling right now," he said gently.

Emily stirred and looked up at the detective. "The other officer said the same thing, but I don't think you can understand how I feel." She shifted in her chair, leaning toward him, and the words shot out of her as if a tab had just been pulled from a shaken soda can. "You've never had to live a life in fear of losing everything dear to you. Seeing them disappear into thin air, like magic—and then not remembering what you did with them or where they went."

Avellino tried to interject, but Emily went on. "You haven't had to endure the frustration of being kicked out of first grade for being a danger to yourself and the other students. And your father probably didn't abandon you after promising that he wouldn't miss your first day of school or your sixth birthday for anything in the world. No doubt you didn't spend your childhood going to the psychologist every week, doing mental exercises to prevent the disappearances from happening again and then waking up every morning hoping that the one thing, that little cherished object received the day before, is still on your nightstand . . . or hanging on the wall."

She took a deep breath, and just when Avellino thought she was done, Emily choked down a sob and cried, "And, for sure, you haven't had to experience the most amazing day of your life spent with the person you love most, the first person who truly understood you, followed by waking up the next morning to discover that he has been murdered, and that, most likely, you are the one who killed them. No, Detective, you can't *possibly* understand what I am feeling right now."

Frank Avellino bowed his head, feeling his chest tighten in sympathy. "You're right, Emily. I haven't experienced those things, but I'm no stranger to pain. I have a son your age. My wife and I adopted him after his parents were killed in a car accident. He was in the car with them. Miraculously, he was unharmed, but the poor boy, just six years old, had to endure hours in the wreckage beside their mangled bodies before anyone discovered the accident. I was the first to arrive at the scene. Peter's dad had been a good friend of mine, and I knew he had no other relatives. My wife and I had always wanted a child but couldn't due to some strange twist of fate, so we decided to adopt him. Peter spent many years in therapy overcoming that trauma. He didn't speak for years. And because of that, he couldn't make friends, and school was always a challenge. My wife and I felt his pain, and we lived through it with him, for many, many years. But today he's doing well. Love can overcome anything."

Emily stared for a moment, then flashed a sympathetic smile. "I'm sorry, Detective," she whispered.

"No need to apologize," Avellino said lightly. "I told you this story because, while the situation may be different, I do understand what you're going through and what you will have to face in the future. But you're young, and life still has a lot in store for you. Trust me."

Emily lowered her head and looked at her still trembling hands. "I dreamed of going to Yale," she whispered. "Instead, I'm going to prison. That's what life has in store for me."

"No, Emily," Avellino reassured her. "You won't go to prison. You aren't the one who murdered your boyfriend."

* * *

Mrs. Barton didn't flinch upon hearing White's words. She showed no surprise or sorrow at the news. She had just heard that her husband had been found dead, and it hadn't seemed to affect her. "What are you trying to tell me, Detective?" the woman asked calmly.

"What I'm trying to tell you, Mrs. Barton, is that you'd better tell us the truth. Make things easier for yourself. Tell us why. Why Albert, and why Robert?" Detective White narrowed his eyes, his confusion apparent.

Valerie remained silent and averted her gaze to the floor, offering no response.

White shook his head, then fixed his gaze on the seemingly unperturbed woman. It was clear in her eyes—the coldness, the unnatural composure, the lack of any emotion, even upon learning that her husband had been dead for years. *But why?* White wondered. Finding the answer to that question would be the prosecutor's job during the trial.

A trial for double homicide.

At that point, Detective White stood up. "You have the right to remain silent, Mrs. Barton. I'm placing you under arrest. Anything you say from now on can and will be used against you in a court of law. You have the right to an attorney during questioning, and if you can't afford one, one will be provided for you." He unholstered the handcuffs from his duty belt.

Valerie stood up, expressionless, a vacant look in her eyes. She extended her wrists, allowing herself to be handcuffed. "Can I see my daughter?" she asked suddenly.

White hesitated. "I don't think that's appropriate, Mrs. Barton."

Valerie's face turned crimson, and she glared at him with unvarnished hatred.

White escorted the woman to the official interrogation room, secured her handcuffs to the metal table in the center of the room, and then left to initiate the necessary arrest procedures.

In the hallway, he passed by the room where Emily was still talking with Frank Avellino. He stopped and studied the girl. He thought about her anguish over the loss of her boyfriend and how that would be compounded when she discovered that her mother, most likely, had killed the poor boy. The same mother who had led her to believe her father had abandoned her. But White believed there was still much to understand. The facts of the matter were still vague, not only the motive for Robert's murder but also Emily's involvement, if any. The detective wondered if Emily was just another victim or if there something dark that needed to be uncovered.

White knew that the investigation was only just beginning, and Valerie's arrest wasn't enough to explain what was hidden in the Barton family's life. He also knew that, without more evidence, there was a risk that the judge might not confirm the arrest.

* * *

Almost an hour passed before Anthony White completed all the arrest procedures for Valerie Barton and then joined Frank Avellino and Emily. It was nearly midnight, and it had been a long day for everyone.

The detective found the girl sipping on a fruit juice, the only thing he'd seen her put in her stomach since the afternoon. White looked at her, her eyes bloodshot and puffy. He wanted to spare her, for now, the news of the likely discovery of her father's remains.

"Emily, unfortunately, we've decided to detain your mother, accusing her of Robert's murder," White began.

The young girl's eyes widened, incredulous. "My mother?" she asked, her voice breaking with horror.

"We have evidence that leads us to believe your mother may be involved in Robert's murder," White explained.

Emily looked around, openly bewildered. "I don't understand."

"We'll explain everything in due time," Avellino interjected. "But right now, I think it's best for you to get some rest. Do you have any relatives who can take care of you until we get to the bottom of all this?"

"I have an aunt," Emily replied, her gaze lost in the void. "Aunt Anna. But she lives in Florida."

"Anna Barton?" White asked.

"No, Detective. Anna Davidson. My mother's sister."

Avellino frowned. "When was the last time you heard from her?"

"I've never spoken to her," Emily said. "But my mother calls her quite often. They are very close."

"Frank, see if you can track down Emily's aunt," White requested as his colleague stood up and swiftly left the room.

White turned his gaze back to the young girl and weighed his next words. "Emily," he said gently, "in the meantime, could you describe your relationship with your mother?"

Emily lowered her gaze to the table, as if searching for the right words to respond. "My mother and I are very close, ever since my father left us."

"When did you find out your father had left?"

Emily responded easily, as if the memory was still fresh. "One morning, eleven years ago. I heard my mother crying, so I went downstairs. I found her in the kitchen, crying, holding my father's goodbye letter."

"Did you ever read that letter?" White asked.

"No, I was only six. I asked my mother to read it to me, but she said no . . . to spare me further pain."

White hesitated again. "And when did your memory loss episodes begin?"

"Right after that. First a doll, then a hairbrush. A chocolate bar, and then that incident at school that forced me to continue my lessons from home."

"What incident, Emily?" White asked, curious.

Emily frowned.

"I'm not sure exactly what happened. One day, as we were leaving the classroom with my classmates, we discovered that two of my classmates' jackets, pink like mine, had been destroyed with shearing scissors or something. When I got home, my mother told me I couldn't go to school for a while. That *while* turned into all five years of elementary school. During that time, she took me to a psychologist, and I spent seven years, every Monday afternoon, talking to Dr. Jackson."

At that moment, Avellino reentered the room, holding a printed sheet of paper. He sat down next to White, his expression a mixture of sadness and frustration, and handed the paper to his colleague.

The detective read the content and narrowed his eyes. "Emily, Detective Avellino conducted a search to locate your Aunt Anna."

"You found her?" Emily asked curiously.

"Yes, Emily. But not in Florida."

* * *

Valerie was placed in a holding cell at the Groton Police Station, awaiting her meeting with the judge the next morning. The judge would decide whether to formally charge her with the murders of Robert Smith and her husband, Albert.

She hadn't confessed to anything, nor had she denied anything. Valerie had listened to Detective White's words without flinching. Even the news of her husband's documents being found on a corpse in the same well where Robert had been discovered didn't faze her.

The woman had one certainty, and it made her strong—the certainty that everything she had done over the years was to raise and protect Emily, her child.

Valerie looked around the cell. It was a small room, about three by four meters in size, containing a cot, a sink, and a toilet. There were no windows, and the only light came from the neon fixture in the hallway on the other side of the bars. It was a temporary holding cell. If she were charged with murder, she would likely end up in a women's prison, and there was a high probability she would spend the rest of her life there.

* * *

"Is Aunt Anna *not* in Florida?" Emily asked, confused.

"No, Emily," Avellino replied. "Anna Davidson, Valerie Davidson's twin sister, died in 1974, at the age of seven, due to a domestic accident."

Panic flooded Emily's mind. "Died? That can't be possible. You must have the wrong person. My mother talked to her less than a week ago! I heard her with my own ears! There must be a mistake!"

White bowed his head over the table, even more confused than he had been a moment before.

"There's no mistake, Emily. I'm sorry," Avellino continued.

There was a moment of silence. White could feel they were each trying to process this information in their own way. To make sense of it.

Within twenty-four hours, Emily had lost her boyfriend, had heard that her mother was accused of his murder, and discovered that her aunt, the only person her mother had been in contact with for years, had actually died thirty-seven years earlier.

"Emily, there's more," said White, looking at the girl tenderly, knowing this would be the final blow.

"What could be worse than what you've already told me?" the young woman demanded, clearly unmoored.

White lowered his head again. "In the well where Robert's body was found, the skeleton of a man was also discovered. In the pants pocket was a wallet, presumably belonging to the victim." He spoke very slowly, trying to be as gentle as possible in delivering that news.

"And who is it?" Emily asked, her tone almost disinterested.

"Your father," White concluded.

Emily froze, then covered her ears. She seemed to have surpassed the point of tears, as if she had no room left for any more pain. She stared into White's eyes, stiff and expressionless, as if she hadn't heard those words.

White sensed her confusion, her terror. The truth of her life, her points of reference, her certainties—everything had collapsed before her, like a house of cards. The young woman remained silent, didn't comment on what he'd just told her, and didn't ask questions.

White knew that this had to be the worst day of Emily's life. What had happened to her, what she had learned, and the pain inflicted on her in the last twenty-four hours had to be difficult to handle psychologically. And he knew that the girl would need a lot of help from that moment on.

"Emily," Avellino said suddenly, after a few minutes of strained silence, "you can stay with my wife and me tonight. My son is out of town, and my wife would be thrilled to have some company for a couple of days."

"Are you sure, Frank?" White asked, turning to his colleague.

"Absolutely," Avellino concluded.

The two men exchanged a look that said they knew that the best thing at that moment would be to keep an eye on Emily. There were still many hidden aspects of the story, and, most importantly, Emily's involvement in the whole affair still needed to be clarified.

The young woman didn't object. "I need to stop by home to get some changes of clothes first," she murmured.

White and Avellino exchanged glances again.

"I'll escort her," Avellino whispered to his colleague.

White thought for a moment before responding. "Okay, Emily. But Detective Avellino will accompany you inside. You'll only retrieve the essentials from your room. Okay?"

Emily nodded.

* * *

Less than an hour later, when Frank Avellino parked in front of the Barton's house, Emily looked out the front passenger side window, silent and staring. Her mind was so crowded with thoughts that they all melded together into a vague gray lump of despair.

The detective opened the car door for her and escorted her to the entrance. The red flag was up on the mailbox, which was affixed to the house beside the door, indicating that there was mail inside. Instinctively, Emily reached out to check the box, then stopped and looked for Frank's permission. He gestured that she could check. There was a letter inside, addressed to her, from Yale University in New Haven.

Emily stared at it. "It's for me. It's a letter that will tell me whether or not I'm getting enough needs-based aid to attend Yale in the fall."

The detective nodded for her to hold on to it.

She slipped it into the back pocket of her jeans, and they went inside. The house felt eerily still. They went up to her room, where she retrieved some clothes from her drawers and put them in her school gym bag.

Back on the first floor, Emily stopped at the door leading to the basement. "Can I see the room where my corsage was found?" she asked.

Avellino took a deep breath and lowered his head. "What's in that room that interests you?" he asked.

"It's just that it's always been locked. My mother said my father took the key with him when he left. I just want to see it, out of curiosity."

Avellino took a moment to think it through. "I suppose it couldn't hurt. It *is* curious. But you can't *touch* anything in there."

Emily nodded and headed down the creaky steps. Once in front of the door, she took a deep breath and waited for the detective to open it. When he pulled the chain on the single-bulb light affixed to the wall inside, Emily stepped forward. Her hand flew to her mouth.

Her eyes drank in the confusing, distressing scene for what seemed like an eternity. "Why?" she finally whispered.

"Why what, Emily?" the detective asked.

"Why didn't anybody notice what was going on in this house? My teachers. My schoolmates. The neighbors. My *therapist . . .*"

Avellino put his hands in his pockets. "People barely recognize their own problems. Hard to see what's going on in other people's homes."

Emily backed out of the room, determined never to step foot inside that horrifying tomb again. She raced up the stairs and out the door. The aluminum screen slammed behind her.

Moments later, they were on the way to the detective's home in Madison, a thirty-minute drive away.

Emily didn't say a word throughout the journey, contemplating Detective White's last words. A man's skeleton had been found with her father's documents in his pocket, in the same well where Robert had been found. It couldn't be a coincidence. That was why her mother had been arrested, the connection between the two victims.

Why? she wondered. *Why kill my father? Why make me believe for all those years that he had abandoned me? Why let me live in hope of his return day after day, year after year? Why make me believe that Aunt Anna was still alive and tell me that she was talking to her on the phone? And why kill Robert?*

It didn't make sense to Emily. Everything that had happened was connected to one thing. And that thought sent a shiver down her spine.

Frank Avellino parked in front of his home. As Emily stepped out, pain shot through her leg.

"Is there something hurting you, Emily?" he asked, frowning at her foot.

“It’s my ankle,” she replied as she followed the detective to the front door. “This morning, coming down the stairs, I tripped over a pair of old boots my mother uses for gardening. But it hurts less now.”

The detective settled Emily into the room his son usually occupied and handed her two towels. Mrs. Avellino had changed the sheets as soon as he’d informed her they would have a guest that night. Then Avellino wished her goodnight and left.

Emily found herself alone for the first time since that morning. She lay down on the bed, still fully clothed, took the letter from her pocket, and opened it. She stared at it, managing to read only the first line before the tears in her eyes blurred the rest.

“Emily Barton, we are happy to inform you that you qualify for full tuition, including room and board, for the upcoming semester.”

Emily let her arms drop. Everything she had dreamed of and worked for had finally come true. She would be going to Yale, a prestigious university where she could pursue her passion. But after everything that had transpired that day, Emily felt no joy. And, at that moment, she realized she may never be happy again.

Chapter 12

YALE UNIVERSITY
NEW HAVEN, CONNECTICUT
AUGUST 29, 2013

Emily stopped in the middle of the New Haven Green, in front of the Harkness Tower, the impressive Gothic-style bell tower rising over the central entrance to Yale University, and gazed up to admire the beauty of the structure. Under her arm, she held a folder with the documents necessary to complete the admission procedures and start attending classes in the following days. The clock above showed exactly nine o'clock.

At that moment, her phone rang. Emily took the phone out of her pocket, smiled at the name on the caller ID, and answered. "Hello!"

"Hi, Emily," replied a male voice from the other end.

Her heart fluttered and she felt her cheeks flush. "Hello, Peter."

"I just wanted to wish you good luck for today," Peter told her.

"Thank you. I really appreciate it."

There were a few seconds of silence.

"I was thinking of taking you out to dinner tonight to celebrate," Peter continued, with a hint of embarrassment. "If you're up for it, I could come by around six, and then we could go to one of those pubs the college students like."

Emily had spent a lot of time in the Avellino's home until she found a permanent arrangement. Frank and his wife had welcomed her as a daughter and had supported her throughout her mother's murder trial, which lasted only a few weeks and was followed by all the national newspapers and broadcasters. Throughout the trial, Valerie had consistently denied killing Robert and Albert. But the jury had no doubts, and after only half an hour of deliberation behind closed doors, the twelve jurors had decided to convict her of both murders.

The murder weapon that had killed Robert had never been found, but the DNA analysis on the bloodstains in the van, the garage, and on Emily's corsage had incriminated Valerie, as had the fact that the two bodies had been found in the same location.

Valerie Barton had been sentenced to life in prison and was incarcerated at York Women's Penitentiary in Niantic, halfway between Mystic and New Haven. This allowed Emily to visit her mother a couple of times a month.

Emily, for her part, had been declared innocent of any involvement in the crimes. All accusations of being an accomplice to Robert's murder had been dropped. It had been proven that the mud on her dress had come from tripping over the boots that morning, which had caused a slight ankle sprain.

After the trial, Emily had reluctantly sold the rights to a documentary and a book about the case. She had accepted interviews and attended various presentations celebrating what had become a bestselling story. She had been heavily criticized for this, but she had needed financial support to continue her studies without having to get a job, which might have impacted her ability to study and maintain high grades.

In the meantime, Emily had gotten to know Peter, Frank's adopted son. The young man had decided to follow in his father's footsteps and enroll in the police academy. They had become friends right away, but eventually, Peter had confessed to feeling something deeper for her. However, Emily hadn't felt ready to start dating him.

Still, Peter had become important to Emily, too, over time, and receiving that dinner invitation had made her happy.

"Of course, Peter!" Emily said with a smile. "That would be great. I'll be waiting for you tonight."

Chapter 13

Mystic, Connecticut
August 26, 2019

Stunned by the sight before him, Peter squeezed Emily's fingers as she slipped her hand into his.

The young man's gaze roamed around the room, taking stock of everything: the floor scattered with various toys, including a creepy baby doll, gift-wrapped packages, a table laden with random objects—a brush, a pair of pinking shears with pieces of pink cloth arranged around it, a petrified chocolate bar, pens, pencils, markers, crayons, a magnifying glass, hairpins, bows, and more.

"You know, Peter," Emily said softly, "it was your father who first entered this room. This is where he found my corsage."

Peter didn't respond, absorbed in slowly circling the room. "Is this your mother and her sister?" he asked, stopping in front of a framed picture on the wall, depicting two smiling little girls.

"Yes," Emily replied sadly. "Aunt Anna. She died at the age of seven. As the news article from the time states, my mother accidentally knocked Anna down the stairs. She broke her neck and died instantly. My mother's mother had been out shopping and had left the girls alone to play in their room. When she returned an hour later, she found my aunt in my mother's arms."

"Why, Emily?" Peter asked, his gaze scanning the gloomy space and stopping on Emily's face. "Why did your mother do all this to you?"

Emily grimaced. "I've spoken with my therapist a lot about this. We concluded it was all about control. Some warped sense of protection. Everything exploded when my father asked for a divorce and requested custody of me. So, in a panic and rage, she stabbed him in the back. That's what the prosecutor's attorney hypothesized during the trial. Then she loaded the body into the cargo bed of the pickup and disposed of it while I was sleeping. She probably threw it from that corner of the road, right into that damn well. Then, when she got back home, she sat at the kitchen table and cried about it. I'll never forget waking up to that cry. I went down the stairs and almost tripped over the muddy boots that, I think, she used to go to the river. I found her sitting at the table, reading and rereading what was supposed to be my father's farewell letter. That was the first lie."

"What lie?" Peter asked, bringing his gaze back to the girl.

Emily looked at the floor, and Peter realized they had never delved so deeply into the story before. "When I saw her crying, I asked her what was wrong. She said my father had left us and that it was his goodbye letter. But the police later discovered that those papers my mother had kept in her dresser all along were divorce papers, dated the day before my father's disappearance. It wasn't a farewell letter. Even the lawyer who had drafted the divorce request for my father had tried to contact him several times at the time. I remember that I once answered one of his phone calls."

"And why all this?" He swept a hand out, encompassing the room. "What are all these things scattered around the room for?"

Emily's tone turned bitter. "My mother feared losing me. That something might happen to me. Or that, one day, I would want to leave her, too. So, she made me believe I had a serious problem. It was a cruel and diabolical way for her to keep me under her control. Of making me feel like I needed her and her protection. The things in this room . . . this is *everything* I cared about over the years and that she systematically made disappear. Like she wanted to be the only one at the center of my world. She put me inside a glass box that I couldn't perceive and from which she didn't intend to let me out. I was in a prison I couldn't see."

"Are *all* these things yours?" Peter asked, growing more curious by the second.

"They *were* mine at one time," Emily replied, looking down. "She made them all disappear—all except for those pink jackets she destroyed. She didn't make *those* go missing. That's how she figured she could make school, which I loved so dearly, disappear, too."

Peter listened, though he'd heard the story before.

"When the school's director testified at my mother's trial, he said they'd caught her vandalizing the jackets on video and demanded an explanation. She said she was trying to prove how lax the school was with their security and how much she feared for my safety there. She paid them cash for the damaged jackets and said she wouldn't bring the story to the local news. To avoid bad publicity, the school brushed the incident under the rug and promised to destroy the video. My mother took me out of the school, claiming to them that it just wasn't safe for me to be there."

"But why wouldn't she want you to go to school?" Peter pressed.

"My therapist and I concluded that it was because she realized that I was making friends and bonding with my teachers and my attention was shifting away from her. She did everything she could to box me in to keep me close to her. She thought she was keeping me safe."

There was a moment of silence.

Peter walked around the room, letting his fingers drift over things without actually touching them, as if this was still a crime scene he didn't want to contaminate. This room was stacked with evidence of a crime against a child, a robbery of her childhood, her father, her boyfriend.

"And it was the same with Robert," Peter mused, looking back at Emily. "Your feelings for him were risking driving you away from her, forcing her to kill him."

Emily nodded miserably. "And that's why I feel responsible for his death. I killed Robert the moment I walked into the house and told my mother that I loved him. She understood at that moment that I would do anything to stay with him. And she was right. That night, for the first time, I felt that Yale and all my future plans had taken a backseat. That I would follow him to the ends of the earth. Or at least, that's what I felt that evening. An evening when I was truly happy and felt, for the first time, normal and unconditionally loved."

"You mustn't feel responsible," Peter almost whispered, repeating the phrase for what seemed like the thousandth time. "A young person has the right to feel those kinds of emotions. It was her. And you must have been very strong to forgive your mother for all this."

Emily grimaced again. "It's not about forgiveness. My mother is sick. She has been since my aunt died. Back then, her parents were too ignorant to understand that she needed therapy after that tragedy. She never got over that loss to the point where she staged, consciously or not, the weekly phone calls with her sister. My father understood it, and perhaps for a while, he tried to live with her problem. Until he couldn't take it anymore. And he asked for a divorce, wanting to take me away from her. But you know how that ended. What my mother did to me is just the consequence of her disorder. Of what happened to her years before." Emily approached the table in the center of the room and starting to fiddle with a pen lying there. "Unfortunately, she has steadfastly maintained her innocence and has passed every psychological test put before her. But I know just how ill she really is."

"It takes a lot of strength to come to that realization," Peter concluded, embracing her from behind.

Emily sighed and stared at the pen. Then her eyes narrowed, and she brought the pen closer to her eyes, mumbling its inscription aloud, "Paola Ford. Connecticut State Department of Education." Her eyes widened, and her hand started to tremble.

"What's wrong?" Peter asked, feeling her heart pounding against his chest. "Did I say something wrong?"

Emily said nothing, squeezing her eyes shut as if trying to remember.

"Emily, tell me! What's on your mind?" Peter insisted.

The young woman turned and stared at him. "We need to go back to the police station right away!" Emily exclaimed, slipping out of his arms and fleeing the room.

Peter, in disbelief, watched her as she left. "What's going on?"

"I'll explain everything later. I need to make sure of something first!" Emily shouted as she ran up the basement stairs.

* * *

Peter parked the car in front of the Groton Police Station, shut off the engine, and turned to Emily. "Would you please tell me what's going on?" he asked impatiently.

"I'll tell you in a moment," Emily replied as she opened the car door. "I want to check something first. Maybe I'm wrong, and I don't want to alarm you."

Emily hurried into the station and headed to the waiting room, to the wall with missing persons photos. She didn't stop to reply to Hank's greeting. She took the pen out of her pocket, searching among the faces and names hanging on the wall.

There it was. "Oh my God!" she exclaimed softly, gently placing her hand on one of the photographs.

Peter approached and read the notice in a whisper, "Paola Ford. Last seen: December 27, 2001."

Emily turned, and they locked eyes. She showed Peter the pen.

The young man read the name on the pen, and his eyes widened. "Do you think . . ."

Emily tore the photo from the wall and sat down in one of the chairs. Peter followed and sat down next to her. She stared at the photo on her lap for a few seconds.

"Ms. Ford was the first one to give me homeschooling lessons after the jacket incident," Emily said quietly, caressing the smiling face imprinted on the paper. "And after that first Christmas, at the end of the year, she gave me this pen and a journal as a gift. It was the last time I saw her."

"But why would your mother kill her?" Peter asked, confused.

Emily gave him a sarcastic smile. "Because I liked her," she replied, shaking her head. "Because I had grown attached to her. Because she gave me a gift, and I was happy about it."

Peter got up from the chair and began to pace. "What should we do now?" he asked, turning toward Emily.

Emily reflected without ever taking her eyes off the photograph. "Last seen December 27, 2001," the young woman whispered as a tear streamed down her face. "Her family and the police have been searching for her for eighteen years."

"We have to report this," Peter urged. "If it was your mother, the judge needs to know!

At that point, Emily looked up at him. "No, Peter, please. You must promise me that you'll let me talk to my mother first."

"Why?" Peter replied, whispering to avoid being overheard. "I can't keep this hidden, Emily. I'm a police officer. It's my duty."

Emily rose and cupped Peter's face in her hands. "My mother will *never* confess. She hasn't confessed to the murder of Robert and my father all these years, and she'll never confess to Paola Ford's either. And that woman's family will never have their daughter's body back. They'll never have answers, and they'll never have a grave to mourn."

Peter sighed heavily. "What do you think you'll achieve by talking to your mother?"

"I believe there's a way to make her tell me where Paola Ford's body is. I have to try," Emily pleaded.

Peter spread his arms in frustration.

"Peter, please," the young woman implored. "Let me try. Please. If she doesn't confess right away, then you can inform the department."

Peter raised his eyes to the ceiling and sighed again. His brow furrowed, and he took a few steps across the room and then returned, stopping in front of Emily. "Okay," he said and pulled her into an embrace. "We'll go back to the prison tomorrow. Unfortunately, I doubt your mother will tell you anything, but I understand that you want to try. After you speak to her, I must bring this information to my superiors."

"Thank you," Emily said, burrowing more deeply into his arms.

* * *

It was eleven in the morning when Peter and Emily parked in front of the prison.

"Thank you for giving me this opportunity," Emily said as she unbuckled her seatbelt.

"You know I'd do anything for you," Peter replied, staring out of the windshield toward the prison entrance. "But, honestly, Emily, you're asking a lot. My job would be on the line if someone were to discover that I withheld this information."

"I understand, but I feel like I'm the best chance of getting some closure for that poor woman's family."

Peter nodded.

Emily got out of the car and followed the same scorching path she had taken the morning before. She went through the various visitor procedures, known to her by heart after all these years, and sat in the same waiting room, in the same spot as the morning before, waiting to be called to meet her mother. She searched for the chipped tile she had seen previously, found it with her gaze, fixed her eyes on it, and started counting.

"One, two, three . . ." Emily stopped. She squinted, took a deep breath, and smiled.

At that moment, she decided that this habit, the exercise she had learned years ago, was no longer necessary. It had never served her; the things she cared about had disappeared all the same. They'd disappeared when her mother had needed to assert her power over her. And she was still succeeding. After all those years, Emily still felt that power pressing down on her. But now, things had changed.

"Barton!" the female security guard shouted.

Emily jumped up, turned, and walked toward the barred door. It was her turn, which meant her mother had agreed to see her.

The girl stopped in front of the iron grate, waiting for it to open, and steadied herself.

Just then, a father and child exited the visitation room just ahead. Maybe their respective wife and mother was an inmate. The child looked miserable as he allowed himself to be led by the hand as if he didn't want that moment to end.

Emily smiled at him as he passed by.

"Barton! Follow me," the corrections officer almost yelled as she motioned for Emily to follow her. "Sit at table seven. Valerie will be here in a moment."

The young woman sat down and placed her hands on the table, suddenly anxious about this confrontation. Her confidence in the success of this operation began to waver when she saw her mother enter. Valerie's face was stern. She was clearly still angered by Emily's news of the day before.

Valerie sat down without looking at her daughter, her eyes fixed on one side of the table. "Why are you here?" the woman asked.

Emily stared at her mother. "Mom, I've thought a lot about what you told me yesterday. I've come to tell you that I might decide not to take the job in Michigan and stay."

Those words piqued the woman's interest, and she turned her gaze to her daughter. "Why?" Valerie asked with a skeptical tone.

"Because I want to make a deal with you," Emily replied. "If you accept, I won't leave and will stay in Connecticut. I'll find a job here, so I can continue to visit you, as usual."

"What kind of deal?" Valerie asked, palpably intrigued.

Emily's pulse pounded in her ears. "A deal where you tell me where Paola Ford is," the young woman whispered.

Hearing this, Valerie's eyes narrowed. For a moment, Emily saw surprise in her mother's eyes. She had intentionally avoided using the term "corpse" or "body." She understood her mother's psychology; over the years, she had realized that her mother's denial of her responsibility in those murders was, in fact, a psychological rejection of her own actions.

"I don't know what you're talking about, young lady," the woman replied.

"I just want to know where she is," Emily insisted. "Nothing else. If you tell me, I'll do as promised. Otherwise, I'll get up and leave. Forever."

"Why are you asking me this?" Valerie asked.

"Because I want her to somehow reunite with her family," Emily replied. "No one deserves this."

There were a few seconds of silence. Valerie looked around as if she were searching for the right words within the walls of that room.

"Mom, please," Emily begged in a whisper, laying her hands on the table between them. "I've never asked you for anything. After everything, I still came here twice a month to visit you. I gave you my love despite everything. But now, I'm asking you for this. And it will stay between us."

Valerie glanced at the table next to theirs. Emily followed her look and saw there were still crayons and sheets of paper that the child had left during his visit lying on the surface.

Valerie reached over to grab a crayon and paper, but her hand hung midair when a guard stepped forward to stop her. Likely realizing Valerie could do no harm with the art supplies, the guard waved her on permissively.

Valerie took what she needed and scribbled something on the paper in red crayon. She then looked up at Emily and handed it to her.

Emily hastily folded the paper and tucked it into the neckline of her dress.

Valerie looked heavenward with the expression of someone who had just relieved a heavy burden. Paola Ford had vanished eighteen years earlier, and Emily knew that years of police investigations had yielded nothing but that Paola's family had never stopped hoping and searching. They had likely issued appeals and offered rewards, but those efforts had led nowhere. Until now.

Emily got up. She looked down at her mother and smiled. "I wish you a peaceful life, Mom. This is goodbye."

"Goodbye?" Valerie repeated, shocked. "You told me that-"

"I lied," Emily interjected. "It's my turn to do the lying, my turn to make decisions for myself. You controlled my life for years, and I forgave you for it. I did it because I know you need help. It's not all your fault. And I hope that one day you admit the truth and seek that help. But I can't sacrifice my dreams because that won't bring you peace. It's time for me, after all this time, to look forward and stop feeling responsible for what *you've* done."

Emily turned toward the exit. As she walked away, the young woman felt her mother's eyes boring into her back, as if they were piercing her heart.

Stepping out into the parking lot, Emily sighed, feeling alive for the first time since the terrible day her father had disappeared.

Chapter 14

MADISON, CONNECTICUT
AUGUST 29, 2019

Emily was in her room, packing her bags, when she heard Peter call her name from downstairs. His tone sounded urgent.

"I'm coming, my love!" she replied, letting the things she was holding in her hands fall onto the bed.

Emily rushed downstairs and found Peter standing in the living room, staring at the television mounted above the fireplace. The screen displayed an aerial shot of Groton Lake, panning over a gathering of people, including uniformed officers, forensic experts, and police divers. The camera was focused on a car that had clearly been hauled up to the lake's surface from deep below.

The news anchor's voice spoke over the video. "This morning, at the bottom of Groton Reservoir, the car of Paola Ford, a young teacher who disappeared in December 2005, was found . . ."

Hearing the journalist's words, Emily touched Peter's hand, and he closed it tightly around hers. Both stared at the screen.

"The case that has left the entire state police in the dark for over seventeen years is shrouded in mystery," the anchor continued. "It seems an anonymous tip came into the Groton Police last night . . ."

Peter turned to Emily with a grave look.

"Peter, believe me," Emily said, embracing him tightly. "This is for the best. My mother is already serving a life sentence, whether she's found guilty of this murder or not. On the other hand, I couldn't bear another trial. More publicity. Interviews and paparazzi. I've finally moved on, and after all these years, there are still people who photograph or film me while I'm at the supermarket. And you saw how Robert's mother treated me at the cemetery. I can't take more of this."

Peter's hand stroked her back, and Emily pulled back to meet his eyes.

"I just want to move forward," she murmured as a tear streaked down her face. "Look ahead. Get married, have a family, and live a normal life."

The anchor's voice cut in again. "Our correspondent on the scene has just informed us that a body has been found inside the car . . ."

Emily and Peter turned back to the television. The helicopter footage now showed police officers covering the car with a white sheet to prevent it from being filmed.

"It's her," Emily said, voice shaking. "She's been at the bottom of that lake all these years."

* * *

The following day, every news channel confirmed that the body found in the car was indeed that of Paola Ford. However, due to the condition of the corpse, which had been reduced to a skeleton and corroded by time and the lake's water, it was impossible to determine the exact cause of death. The most plausible hypothesis was that the young woman had lost control of the car and ended up at the bottom of the lake. But there remained the mystery of the anonymous phone call that had led the police to discover the body. Who had made the call? And why after all these years? Experts and journalists asked this question hour by hour.

Emily knew there would never be an answer. A few days later, she moved to Michigan and began her job at Pfizer. In the years that followed, she never stepped foot in York Women's Prison again.

Chapter 16

PELHAM, NEW YORK
JULY 1, 2023

After two years of working in Michigan, Emily had transferred to the company's headquarters in New York, as the couple had hoped would be the case. He had transferred to the Greenwich Police Department in Connecticut the year before. Shortly after, she and Peter had a small wedding in the spacious backyard of Peter's childhood home. The couple bought a lovely three-bedroom home halfway between their workplaces, and nine months later, they had a baby girl: Paola Avellino.

Emily had stayed abreast of any developments in Paola Ford's case, but there had been little to no progress. She felt that in some small way that naming her daughter Paola would bring her teacher peace beyond the grave. She also kept abreast of her mother's ongoing appeal case, but the chance of Valerie being found not guilty of the murders was slim to none. There was simply too much evidence implicating her.

It was a warm, quiet Saturday morning, and Peter sat in his leather recliner in the living room reading the news on his iPad, while Emily and two-year-old Paola sat on the carpet building a Lego house.

At 11:00 a.m., Peter's text chime broke the quiet. Emily glanced up to see Peter peering at his phone in confusion.

"Who is it?" she asked, affixing two of the smaller Legos together.

"My dad," Peter replied, grabbing the remote from the coffee table in front of him. "He said to turn on the TV to NBC."

Emily quickly glanced at Peter, her brow furrowed, and then looked at the television screen. A shiver ran down her spine, and she had a terrible sense of foreboding.

The television screen showed a journalist standing at the entrance of the Hartford Courthouse in Connecticut and speaking into a microphone. "Finally, this morning, a verdict has been reached in Valerie Barton's appeal case against the double murder of her husband, Albert Barton, and seventeen-year-old Robert Smith, a case that lasted nearly two years. In 2011, Valerie Barton was sentenced to life without parole, but the defendant has always maintained that she was innocent of the two murders. The story, at the time, caused a great sensation, inspiring a documentary and a bestselling book. . ."

Emily and Peter stood, eyes glued to the screen. Paola continued playing with the Legos, seemingly oblivious that anything was wrong.

"Today, however," continued the journalist, "thanks in part to the defense of attorney Gregory Penn, who became well known in the nineties for defending the Savannah Killer, that verdict has been overturned. In fact, the appeals court jury has declared Valerie Barton *not* guilty of the two crimes based on a technicality related to the collection of evidence . . ."

Emily put her hand to her mouth in terror.

"I'll now pass it over to my colleague Peter Steel, who is currently outside the York Women's Correctional Facility," the journalist concluded.

The images onscreen changed to show a different journalist standing outside the prison, backdropped by the familiar entrance Emily knew too well. "Thank you, Mike! As you already mentioned, Valerie Barton was declared innocent this morning based on a technicality related to the collection of evidence. Some are already comparing this case to that of OJ Simpson and crying scandal. And while, a short while ago, Valerie Barton left the York Women's Correctional Facility from a back door, the family of Robert Smith has declared themselves devastated, losing all faith in American justice and the state of Connecticut . . ." The camera focused on the glass door, through which Emily could see the guards standing at the entrance.

Emily approached Peter and hugged him tightly, almost desperately. "I can't believe it," she mumbled, her face pressed against his chest. "I can't believe it."

Peter stroked Emily's hair without responding.

"It's my fault, Peter. It's all my fault. I should have let you tell them."

Peter pointed the remote control at the television and turned it off, filling the room with silence. "No, my love," he said. "It's not your fault. You did what was right for Ms. Ford's family. We could not have foreseen this."

The doorbell rang. Startled, Peter and Emily exchanged a perplexed glance; they weren't expecting anyone. Peter narrowed his eyes, as Emily detached herself from her husband's arms. She went to the door and opened it, knowing full well who would be on the other side.

Valerie smiled at her speechless daughter and then peeked into the living room behind her. "I hear there's a little girl here who needs her grandma's cuddles," she said, sidestepping Emily and making her way into the house, her gaze fixed on the blond, green-eyed child playing on the carpet.

Other Books by the Author available in English:

A One Way Ticket (2022)
Shakespeare: Conspiracy of Silence (2021)

Made in United States
North Haven, CT
06 December 2023

45178383R00117